TM

SHAWN E. FENNELL

Published by Clam Shack Media LLC
USAwww.clamshackmedia.com

ISBN : 0615681573
ISBN 13 : 9780615681573
LCCN : 2012914539

ACKNOWLEDGEMENTS

To the inspirational children, their parents and families – those whose paths I crossed silently and those I became fortunate to know personally and call friend. Corinna, Michael, Michelle, Kyle, Mitzi, Andrew, Tim, Cathy, Brendan, Jake, Kim, Rich – Thank you. You are and will always be my inspiration. I realize and appreciate the courageous example you set each day. My collage of vivid memories - watching you lead by example will never fade over time. You have seamlessly taught me timeless life lessons for which I am a better person, a better friend, a better husband and a better dad.

Thank you to all my family and friends with whom I have discussed the project, and read proofs of the manuscript – thank you for your commitment to our friendship, your candid thoughts and always welcoming me with a smile.

Greg T. – thank you for the push and instilling confidence in this novice storyteller that was known only to his kids at bedtime.

Jon G. – thank you for sharing your love of writing and challenging me to tell a better story. You are an amazing writing coach and editor that helped me find a voice within myself that I can be proud of, so I may fulfill my passion to speak for those who can't.

Mom and Dad – though you have passed away since I began this project, I still feel your spirit and encouragement. Thank you for shaping my life.

Lita, Brooke and Jack – thank you for your love, unwavering trust and excitement these many years. You always listened like it was the first time you were hearing something, with wide eyes. Thanks for your patience, when I often said, "I'll be right there." Your unrelenting faith and confidence in me has inspired me to reach as far as I could … and then a little bit more.

TABLE OF CONTENTS

Chapter 1   Wish Upon Tonight 1

Chapter 2   Bullish Way 5

Chapter 3   Film at Eleven 21

Chapter 4   Care to Dance 35

Chapter 5   Be-Cause 43

Chapter 6   Arms Wide Open 49

Chapter 7   Frost Heaves 69

Chapter 8   Swing Oil 77

Chapter 9   Press or Pull 95

Chapter 10   Dreamsicle 115

Chapter 11   Giddy Up 135

Chapter 12   Tomorrow's Light 155

Chapter 13   Feats 171

Chapter 14   Transom Be Told 189

Chapter 15   Physics of It All 217

Chapter 16   The Call 231

Chapter 17   Plane Water 235

Chapter 18   Doorway to Awareness 247

Chapter 19   Signs 251

Epilogue **257**

CHAPTER 1

Wish Upon Tonight

The old man slogs through virgin snow, dropped fast and furious by a freak, early-season nor'easter that's flogged New England. It's slow going through the wet, knee-high snowpack; it has the clumping consistency of mashed potatoes. He labors to lift his heavy boots and reset his steps as he drags an old sled behind him in short, lurching yanks. He stops, pauses, and lets fall the length of rope from his right hand while taking stock of his surroundings.

The man has little more than three hours left to live, a fact that wouldn't surprise him much if he were to spend any amount of time thinking about it. But time spent thinking doesn't interest him at this point. This trip is about *feeling*.

It's quiet with the muffled silence only a good snow-storm can bring to urban living. A stand of white and red pines along the crest of a hill above him looks as if it's frosted in sugared icing, the dark trunks standing out in solid profile against the whiteness on the ground. It's stopped snowing and the sky is clearing with help of a brisk wind as if a giant broom is sweeping it clean. *It's time,* the old man thinks. *I think I trust this man, Michael, and what he promised. But I'm still a little scared.*

As he picks up the rope and resumes his plodding course through the snow, the exertion causes him to breathe heavily. The sound of his own heart beats a steady bass rhythm in his temples, adding counter rhythms to his gasping exhalations. The old man is slightly alarmed by these very mortal sounds, a remnant survival instinct.

It is midnight now, and as the sky finishes clearing, a bril-liant, milky-white moon, almost full, hangs straight overhead. It's as far from Earth as it will get this night, splitting the dif-ference between dusk and dawn. Steam rises from the man's nostrils, fogging the oversized lenses that have slipped down the bridge of his nose from his exertions. He removes his win-ter gloves to wipe his glasses clean. His left hand is wrapped in a blood-spotted bandage that covers what apparently is a deep wound across his palm. He opens and flexes his hand, wincing a little from the pain. With his right hand, he takes out a handkerchief from his rear pants pocket. He uses it to wipe the lenses clean, puts them back on his face, and exhales slowly through his lightly pursed lips, shooting a vapor trail into the night.

He takes in a deep, deliciously cold breath and holds it to ease the soreness in his throat and lungs. This leads to a wracking cough that involuntarily bends him over at the waist. He heaves as the coughing subsides, and he catches a scoop of phlegm with a deliberate hawking sound from the back of his throat, an offering from deep in his lungs that he draws up and spits out. The fresh, red arterial blood stands out in deep contrast to the pure white snow.

Gut-check time, he thinks, and then he laughs out loud. *Phew! Given I have a belly full of cancer, the term "gut check" is just a wee bit ironic, isn't it now, old man?*

Throat cleared and breath restored, he straightens up and casts his eyes about for a landmark, some point of reference to grant him some perspective on where he's standing. It's a familiar enough place turned alien ground by the presence of the snow. Finally he finds it, an embossed sign nailed into the trunk of an adjacent white pine crusted with wind-driven snow. He looks down at the Flexible Flyer, a relic and cherished reminder of great memories when sledding with his children, and his children's children. *Except for Chas, that is.* He feels himself dip a bit toward melancholy. *Poor kid—never knew what it was like to be swept away by the forces of nature. He'll be all right, though. That's what the man says, after all.*

The old man bends over and wipes the sled's surface free of some snow, an almost perfectly formed snowball that's settled there. *Haven't so much as touched this sled in years*, he thinks, looking down at it. *But it's taking me where I'm supposed to go. The sooner I go, the sooner I'll be back safe in my chair, where I belong.* He looks up the hill and resumes his climb toward the crest.

Somewhere nearby, a dog barks.

CHAPTER 2

Bullish Ways

About seven hours later and three miles away, a tired-looking, faded blue Honda Accord makes its way up Mass Ave and takes a slightly too fast right turn onto Meriam Street. Coughing into a shuddering idle in front of the Adams Building that houses the *Arlington Advocate*, the car pauses to let an early morning bicyclist cross on his way north up the Minuteman Commuter Bikeway, or simply "the bike path," as it is referred to by local Arlingtonians. Putting on a blinker almost as an afterthought, the Honda's driver heaves it into a parking lot just across the bike path from the *Advocate*, and rolls it to a slow stop between a concrete barricade and a late-model Camry. With the killing of the engine, the blaring strains of Wilco's "Art of Almost" are simultaneously struck still, and the driver, a slightly built girl, gets out as a small avalanche of snow from the car's roof cascades onto her head and down the front of her open parka.

"Arrrrrgh!" she growls. "Not fair!" Suddenly self-conscious, she looks around to see if anyone witnessed her outburst. Satisfied that she was unobserved, she reaches into the backseat of the Accord and wrestles an uncooperative backpack out of the car, slings it over her shoulder, and bends back across the front seat to grab her medium-sized Dunkin' Donuts Extra-Extra from the console drink holder. Bumping the backpack into the doorjamb, she is caught up short and more snow falls on her. This time she laughs to herself. "Okay, Klutzcake, get it all out of the way now, thank you very much. Time to impress your internship-ees with your grace and dexterity."

Finally getting her coffee cup, backpack, and keys put into proper places in her left hand, over her shoulder, and in her parka's side pocket, Angie Clarke begins to wind her way into the *Advocate*, careful to place her blue retro Converses into the icy footprints of previous travelers. "Thank God *somebody* has big feet," she says under her breath as she crosses the path and makes her way inside.

Stepping into the newsroom and dropping her backpack into a more comfortable position at her side, Angie looks over at the reception desk and says, "Good morning, Brenda. Sorry I'm a little late."

"Don't worry, dear," Brenda replies. "Not a lot going on yet anyway. Keefe Funeral Home sent over an obit, I think. We have a few online photo requests if you're looking for something to do. Have a nice Thanksgiving?"

"Yup," Angie says. "Mom and Dad think they have to fatten me up for those Syracuse winters. You?"

"Yeah, it was good. Quiet. A divorcée's Thanksgiving is more about being thankful I don't have to watch football all day and smell bad feet while we eat in front of the TV. Speaking of man caves, Mr. Armstrong says he wants to see you in his office as soon as you get in. We've missed you!"

"Good mood or bad mood?" Angie asks.

"What do you think? He's working the day after Thanksgiving. The Pats lost to the Lions. Good luck."

Angie raises her eyes to the ceiling as she threads her way through a bullpen cluster of dented and scarred steel desks, the soles of her sneakers squeaking like tiny ducks on the linoleum floor. Angie picks out her old desk by the permanent stain from the succession of greasy pizza boxes that held her daily lunches over the summer before going off to college. Plopping her backpack into a tired-looking chair, its wounds crisscrossed with frayed and blackened duct tape, she spins with a drawn-out squawk and heads into the office of her editor, Bill Armstrong. She pauses at the door and peeks in, head tilted to one side. Looking up over a computer screen at her, he motions her in with his left hand while cradling a phone between his shoulder and ear. His right hand makes quick, hard swipes impatiently across a mouse pad spotted with coffee stains. The mouse itself is invisible, swallowed whole by Bill's large hand.

"I'm sorry we had to run your son's name in the police reports, Mrs. Jackson," he says into the phone, still moving the mouse around as if conducting a mini symphony on his desk. He listens to the voice, which is loud enough to be almost audible from the receiver. "Yes, I'm sure he *was* influenced by the newer elements in town, too, Mrs. Jackson. We're becoming a little Cambridge, like you say." He rolls his eyes, listens to some more sonic flak. "Yup, a town changes, just like the weather," he says into the phone. "But it seems as if there's always weather and never as many booms. But there's always busts and I'm sorry your Frederick was one of the ones busted for pot down at that party at Menotomy Rocks Park."

He listens again, leans back in his chair, and looks up at the ceiling, rubbing his hand across his forehead. "Mrs. Jackson, we're the paper of record for Arlington, and as such, we record everything from the mundane to the ridiculous to the sublime. One of those things is the police reports. Arrests, miscues, accidents, lost dogs—you name it. We don't write 'em; we report 'em. Everyone from the mayor to the moron who runs this paper. If it makes you feel any better, I once ran my niece's name in the police blotter because, well, because that's where her name was. Had to sleep on the couch for a week, but I slept with a clear conscience."

Armstrong settles back down at his desk, leaning forward on his elbows. "Okay, Mrs. Jackson, I'll cancel your subscription."

Making sure she hangs up first, he likewise hangs up the phone gently as if it were made of porcelain. Bill looks at Angie and shakes his head, as he points to a vacant chair to the left of his desk. "Probably resubscribe in a couple of months once her son gets into a drug diversion program and she feels better about it, but when someone's life spills out on the printed page, they tend to blame the printer. Good to see you, Ms. Angie Clarke. Long time, no see. School going okay?"

"Yes, Mr. Armstrong, I aced my poli-sci and my Ethics in Journalism midterms," Angie answers, taking the proffered seat. "I think those talks we had last summer, about when you were covering Watergate for *The Baltimore Sun* back in the '70s, really helped with the essay part. I even quoted you with your 'Don't pick a fight with someone who buys their ink by the barrel' line."

"Well, Angie, that's why you're one of the best interns we've had around here," Armstrong says with a small chuckle, twisting in his seat to face her, and crossing a pair of beefy forearms poking out of his rolled-up sleeves. "You make sure you remind me how smart I am and we'll continue to get along famously. But the ink-by-the-barrel line was actually Mark Twain, not me. And I thought we got over that 'Mr. Armstrong' thing. You coming back during vacations and breaks makes you almost a staffer, not just a summer intern."

"Are you offering me a job, Mr. Armstrong, uh…Bill?"

"Not yet, young lady. As a fellow Orangeman, I need to remind you Syracuse does not produce dropouts. At least our part, the Newhouse School of Public Communications, doesn't. Tell you what, though—you want a story? I heard something on the scanner about a code 11-44 over at the Winchester Country Club a little earlier. Apparently, some old geezer decided to go sledding. Normally wouldn't be our story, but Chief Braden called and said the guy was a local. So, why don't you head down to Mystic Street and get us a scoop?"

Angie's face loses it color. Shifting in her seat and crossing her right knee over her left, her right hand wanders up to a spot just above and behind her right ear. With an extended forefinger, she sweeps a small section of her shoulder-length, brown-blond hair into a spray that she twists around, and then around again, before finally holding it in a bent form between her forefinger and thumb. She bounces it lightly against the tip of her nose and lets it drop back into place.

"Something eating at you, Angie?"

"Um, I…how do you know I'm agitated?"

"You're twirling and sniffing your hair. Reporters are above all else people watchers. And when we watch people do something that has no practical purpose, there's usually a reason. And since twisting and sniffing your hair has no practical purpose, such as hair maintenance, there's got to be another reason—say, to dispel some nervous energy on your part? Therefore, my guess is, something is agitating you." He tilts his chin and studies her with raised eyebrows, a small, Mona Lisa smile on his lips.

"Well, I don't know, Mr., uh, Bill. It just sounds kind of weird and familiar at the same time, like it happened before or something…you know. I don't know. It just hit me funny, I guess." Angie looks down at her feet and bites her lip. Bill holds his pose and lets the silence sit. After about twenty seconds, Angie continues. "I think I read a similar story about a guy dying sledding somewhere out west, like Montana, earlier this month. I was looking up newspapers around the US to send resumes to when I graduate, and there was some town paper I was reading on the Internet, or maybe it was a blog or something. It just sounds familiar."

"Eck, blogs!" spits Bill, a look of disdain spilling across his face, sour as month-old milk. "Writing a blog doesn't make someone a journalist any more than using a steak knife makes someone a heart surgeon. Don't even talk to me about blogs."

"I know, Bill, I know," says Angie, trying to suppress a grin.

"Well, go check out the local who ended up dead on his sled. See where the story goes," Bill says as he turns back to face his monitor and fiddle with his computer's mouse. Angie gets up, knowing a dismissal when she's given one by her mentor. She moves toward the door before being stopped by Bill.

"So how'd you do with the rest of your courses?" he asks, not looking up from the screen.

"Well, I got a D-plus in Physics 101 and I'm running an incomplete in Statistics. But I'll make it up by the end of the semester," she adds quickly.

"Not so dedicated to the prerequisites, eh, Angie? Two things to keep in mind here. One, it helps to know some of the Universal Laws of Nature you'll learn in physics, and two, not all courses are supposed to be treasure-packed pleasure trips. If they were, they wouldn't have names like 'Statistics.'

It'd be called 'Fun Facts for Frat Rats.' Don't get them confused with the elective classes, like 'Clay for an A.' Bear down, Angie. Employers look at your cumulative average to make sure you can cover the church picnics with as much energy as you can a church fire."

"Okay, Bill, I will. I promise," Angie says as she backs out the door and heads back toward the bullpen.

At her desk, Angie picks up her Extra-Extra and takes a few quick slurps before putting on her coat and grabbing her backpack as she heads toward the newspaper's door. "See you later, Brenda. I'm going to the cop shop to check the ID of a deceased man over in Winchester."

"Alrighty, Lois Lane, you take care," says the comfortably plump, middle-aged receptionist. "We see you later?"

"Probably. I want to log a few hours before I head back to turkey-sandwich heaven. Who knows, there might even be a story here."

"Well, you know what Bill would say about that..."

"Yeah, yeah," Angie answers with a small laugh. "'*Everything* is a story, and every*one* has a story.' I remember the first story assignment he gave me last summer." Adopting a deep voice to imitate her mentor, Angie intones, "Go get a story from someone down at the train station. I don't care who it is, but talk to someone you don't know and find out what it is they do for work, for fun or for others. Find out what makes them tick. Analyze them and take them apart piece by piece. Then put them back together again, using their words and your supporting descriptions so that their lives are something people will want to read about and learn from."

Brenda laughs. "That's our Bill. Tough taskmaster, but a master of tasking nonetheless."

Angie nods. "Yeah, a real-life Yoda with an attitude," she says and goes out to her car.

Arriving at the Arlington Community Safety Building, a two-story mixture of brick and concrete, with a large glass A-frame atrium dividing its two separate parts, Angie parks and goes into the building. At the police dispatchers' booth, she stops and waits for a woman, with dark brown hair swept back into a severe-looking ponytail, manning the front to turn in her direction. "Yes?" asks the woman, still not quite looking at her. "Can I help you?" Finally looking up at Angie, her eyes brighten and her impassivity crests and breaks. "Oh, it's you, the Clarke girl. Where you been? Haven't seen *you* in awhile."

"Well, Officer Beattie, I've been at school. I'm back home for school break. Figured I'd get some work in for the *Advocate.*"

"Couldn't stay away from the curmudgeon, could ya?"

"Mr. Armstrong? He's not so bad," says Angie.

"Maybe not for you because you're still clay to be molded, but the rest of the world he treats as if we're clay pigeons to take potshots at. And all us pigeons have feet of clay." Debby Beattie laughs at her own wit. Angie doesn't laugh. "I see you got your journalist face on, dear. How can I help you?"

"Can I see Chief Braden? We heard there was a dead, er, I mean, deceased man from town found over at the Winchester Country Club."

"That's okay, dear, you can call him 'dead.' He has, after all, ceased being anything. You talking about the dead sledder?"

"Yes. Can I find out anything about who he is and what happened?"

"The chief isn't in, probably out walking around town, hoping to get offered a slice of pie. Tell you what, though. How about I just get up and walk over to the coffee machine and you just happen to lean over my desk and read this not-quite-ready-for-official-release police report? Bill Armstrong taught you to read upside down off of people's desks, didn't he?"

"Nooo. Well, he suggested it might be a good thing to learn," said Angie slowly.

"Well, I can smell that nasty coffee calling, Angie Clarke. Nice seeing you. You be back over Christmas?"

"Yup. I have a whole January term, too, so I guess I'll be doing some more stories. And thanks, Officer Beattie."

"You're welcome. Read fast."

Angie leans through the partition and stretches as far over the desk as she can, picking out the relevant lines to read on the police report. *Victim: Fife, Charles M. DOB: Sept. 20, 1926. Address: 21 Walnut Terrace.* She jots this down in her slim notebook.

> Incident report: Deceased found on south slope on the fairway of the 15th hole of the Winchester Country Club by cross country skier at approx. 6:24 a.m. Police called and deceased found not breathing, with no pulse, on his left side next to a Flexible Flyer sled. Deceased fully clothed and showed no visible signs of distress. Coroner declared deceased dead at the scene at 7:48 a.m.

"Fife...Fife..." Angie says under her breath. "Where do I know that name from?" Distracted, she heads back out of the station. At the front doorway she sees a well-dressed woman, with a long dark coat of some undistinguishable animal fur and a discernable air of impatience, sweep around a young man in a wheelchair, who is having some obvious difficulties getting the door open far enough to get through. Following in the wake of the woman, Angie stops and holds the door for the man, a top-heavy youth with skinny, obviously inert legs, who appears to be in his twenties.

"I don't get some people," says the disgusted youth.

"Yeah, well, maybe she was thinking you could have pushed the handicapped button, so the door opens automatically," says Angie, feeling a sudden flush of guilt for not hiding her own feelings of impatience with the delay.

"Personally, I don't care for the term 'handicapped.' 'Person living with a disability' is better choice, just so you know, and I don't like shortcuts," says the youth. "I find them limiting, and I don't like feeling limited." He wheels through the door, pops a wheelie, and spins right, like a halfback eluding a tackle. He drops down to four wheels and beats a furious pace toward the parking lot.

That was weird, Angie thinks, then dismisses the thought and heads back to her car and the awaiting office.

Back at the *Advocate*, Angie powers up a clunky-looking desktop computer. It makes a low, grinding noise before lurching into action. She looks for a recognizable brand name. *Must have been put together in someone's garage*, Angie mutters to herself, before settling into her seat and clicking icons to get onto the Web and the paper's network server. Angie taps her fingers on the desk and contemplates her next move. She takes a sip of what is left of her Extra-Extra coffee and twirls her hair. She pops up from her desk and rummages through the bookshelves of a couple of her adjacent coworkers. She finds what she's been looking for, an

Arlington phone directory. As she walks back to her desk, she flips through pages, until coming to the Fs.

"I know this name, but from where?" she says to herself. "Oh, now I remember…here it is. Fife. Oh, my God, it's them." Angie reflects on what she knew about the Fife family. *They are such a nice family, and very athletic too. Yeah, he was inducted into the High School Football Hall of Fame and he donated his award to his grandson. I remember that day. What the heck was he doing on a sled, in the middle of the night after Thanksgiving?*

Angie pulls her hair from the back and twirls yet again. As if rehearsing for a role from *The Godfather* movie, she mimics the actor, Al Pacino.

"Just when I thought I was out, they pull me back in." She smirks as her fingers race across the keyboard. Logging into the archives of the newspaper's website and feeling very much like a detective, she begins running all the details and possible scenarios through her mind. *Why was he sledding on Thanksgiving night? And by himself? That is too, too weird. Eighty-five-year-old granddad… heart attack, maybe? And by himself or with someone else? Did they run for help?*

She finds what she's seeking on the server, takes a sip of coffee, and edges her chair closer to the desk. "Ahh, here it is. 'Fife Inducted into Hall of Fame.'" Angie clicks away with her mouse and her eyes run up and down the screen. *Pictured here are the members of the Hall of Fame Fife family. From left to right: Vera; Charles Sr., "The Bull"; Charles II, and Chas.* Angie grabs a lock of hair and twirls again—three quick twists—and then falls motionless, staring at the photo. "Oh my God, that is just so sad. I don't get it. It's all so weird."

"Whataya got, rook?" Bill's voice, like gravel poured onto a table, surprises Angie and she sits back, startled. He is looking over her shoulder. She can smell cigar and aftershave.

"Got the victim's name," she answers. "Charlie Fife, Sr. He was eighty-five."

"Oh, the Fifes," says Bill, straightening up. "They're a big football family. Got a kid in the family with some disease that has him in leg braces, probably a grandson to Old Charlie. That's what everyone calls—called—Charlie Sr. here. He was the late sledder? Doesn't sound like the kind of foolish thing he'd do. No sign of foul play or alcohol, huh?"

"Nothing in the report, Bill."

"Well, write it up as a simple death-by-exposure story. Should be more than just a police report," Bill says, walking away. "Probably get an obit notice from Keefe's or O'Brien's later, too, so write that up as well, 'kay, rook?"

Angie calls out to him, "I want to check out that death in Montana, too, all right, Bill?"

"Go ahead, but it's probably just a coincidence," he says before disappearing into his office.

CHAPTER 3

Film at Eleven

Cold weather comes early to the party in the North Country. There's no gentle transition between the briskness of late fall and the harshness of winter on the frozen tundra of Syracuse University's campus. Old Man Winter just breaks down the door, puts his snowy boot down hard, and leaves it there for the next four months. And then howls an icy laugh that knocks down trees and breaks the human spirit. But it helps students stay in and study, at least some of the time.

Dressed in multiple layers of fleece, flannel, and down, Angie hoists her backpack, weighted as if readied for a thru-hike of the Appalachian Trail. She deftly picks her way across her dorm-room floor, without managing to tip over the strategically placed piles of laundry, books, and plastic bags stocked with munchies. She edges out the door and into the quiet hallway. Taking the stairs, she winds her way down the four floors that lead toward the street level. She is immediately struck by cold air driven colder by a stiff wind, her face feeling flash frozen as if she were a high-end Omaha steak. Spurred to moving quickly to limit her exposure, she hurries out of Sadler Hall and circles the Carrier Dome before cutting through the main campus. Bent against the wind, she comes out onto University Place, which she crosses on her way into the Schine Student Center. Entering the atrium, she looks over at the full-sized orange tree growing there and immediately feels warmer. Veering left, she heads toward the cafeteria where the welcoming smells of fried eggs, bacon, and coffee pull her in like a moth to a flame.

Seeing her friend and roommate Sarah Schwartz, in a far corner surrounded by several other students, male and female but mostly female, Angie heads to their table to deposit her book-laden backpack and her parka. Sarah, a top-heavy, compact blond with black roots reasserting themselves close to her scalp, beckons loudly to Angie when she sees her coming.

"Hey, roomie," booms Sarah. "How ya doin'? Figured I'd letcha sleep in so you'd be rested up for your nine forty-five class." The shores of New Jersey drip from her vowels.

"What do you mean, Sar, let me sleep in? You never came in to sleep in the room last night!" Angie remains standing over the table.

"Well, see, there was this bottle of Absolut and this hunk of absolute beefcake, and…it got late early, ya know what I'm sayin'?"

"Yes, unfortunately, I really do think I know what you're sayin'. I didn't miss the food reference, either." She sits down at the edge of her chair across the table from her roommate and leans forward. "Whom are we talking about when we are referring to someone who is both the protein and the sugar part of the meal?"

"Remember Bus Crush? I saw him at Darwin's, and he saw me and then, well, we saw each other." Several of Sarah's friends hear the exchange and laugh. A few chorus, "Whoo-hoo!"

Angie's face remains impassive as she absorbs this bit of social networking news. Then she shakes her head slowly. "He may be a crush you got on the campus bus, but the way he parties? He's going to look more like beef jerky than beefcake in about five years. Sar, he is a world-class jerk. I not only met him with you, but I've heard about 'mass male-ings' he's put out there. He'd be one of those guys who is totally unaffected by things such as, well, scruples. Heck, he even hit on me while he was hitting on you."

"Ah, Angie, you don't know him. He's really sweet."

"He's a business major. His father owns a chain of restaurants and he's going to help manage them. Sweet? Try saccharine. He's just going to leave you with a bad taste in your mouth."

"Oh, and don't tell me—his father is an alum," says Cathy Brennan, a classmate who also takes journalism classes with Angie. "What kind of restaurant manager could he possibly be? He thinks a Funyun is a vegetable and cream of wheat comes from the mammary glands of, like, wheat."

"Sar, we all just think you can do better," Angie adds. "Remember how he was trying to suck water out of that canteen he wears all the time to look like a mountain man? Well, water freezes in Syracuse, a fact that is a little too complicated for Bus Crush to comprehend."

"Yeah, yeah, funny, Ange, but he treats me nice, and that's important, ya know. He holds the door for me and everything."

"Sarah, he quotes *Conan, the Barbarian*, like, every time we're down at Darwin's," chimes in Cathy. Switching to a low, Arnold Schwarzenegger impersonation, she says, "'More ale, wench, and fresh horses for the men. For tonight, we ride.' Corny!"

Angie picks up the thread of the imitation and they chorus, "'Conan, what is best in life? To crush one's enemies, to see them driven before you, and to hear the lamentations of their women.'" They both collapse into peals of laughter.

Sarah lets out a loud "ha!" and shows a mouthful of teeth before straightening up and composing herself. "Well, at least he isn't a serial killer. That's gotta count for somethin' these days."

"Good to see you set your standards realistically, Sar," says Angie.

"As we say down in Jersey, any port in a storm," answers Sarah.

"Okay, Sar, okay. You do what you want," Angie says. "Just don't bring him into our dorm room for overnights, all right?" She changes the subject. "I'm going to get some breakfast. Anybody want anything?"

"How 'bout a chocolate donut, or maybe start the day with cake? You need some money?" Sarah leans over the edge of the table, displaying a generous amount of cleavage that does not go unnoticed by several neighboring tables.

Angie gives her roommate a look. "I'm buying you a turtleneck for Christmas."

"Chanukah would be a better choice. Hey, Ange, I need a sugar fix," Sara continues, shrugging her shoulders with an exaggerated look of innocence. "What do you think?" Sarah is pointing to an adjacent table of girls who are sharing a chocolate-chocolate cake.

"We shouldn't do it," replies Angie. "Just think—you won't like yourself tomorrow, and it will be yet another battle that the early-morning StairMaster will lose to the late-night Fat Monster. Now, do you really want to disappoint Sir StairMaster again?" she asks.

Sarah puts on a pouting face, with lips puckered up. Angie has seen this act before and caves in every time. Angie disgustingly gets up from the chair. "Whatever. Let's just get through this," she says. "I can tell you right now—we are not having another Dr. Phil episode again tonight back in the room, about your body-fat ratios and your food-intake levels and how you hate yourself because you can't control yourself."

"I promise, Ange, I'll have my cake and eat it for two, and I won't complain in the evening," Sarah says with mock seriousness.

Angie goes and gets herself some breakfast and Sarah some cake, and they hurry through their food so they won't be late for their classes. Sarah and some of the rest of students at the table get up and ready themselves for the bitter Syracuse cold. Cathy and Angie head off last, since the Newhouse School for Public Communication is right next door. Heading toward their class together, they approach the school within a college and Angie is struck, as she is every time, by its edifice. The words of the First Amendment, embedded in a ceramic frit glaze set on the curvilinear glass that wraps around its entirety, serve to remind the students of the importance of the task—delivering the news—they have taken up as their chosen profession.

Angie and Cathy join the other students, filing in to their seats in the open classroom in which their Television Newswriting class is taught. Angie sneaks a look over at Jack Minor, a well-built young man, sitting straight-backed in his chair and holding his notebook down against the table in his left hand, while lightly tapping a Bic pen against the table with his right. Already looking directly at her, Jack smiles and mouths a hello. Flushing lightly, she struggles to not immediately look away in embarrassment, and urges her lips to purse together and tilt them slightly upward. She quickly breaks eye contact and busies herself extracting her notes, pen, and highlighter. Professor Joseph Gemma greets them and gives a brief introductory lecture about how to prepare a spot news piece on deadline, before turning on the large, flat-screen television on the wall above them.

"Here, as usual, is last night's eleven o'clock news," he says once he has everyone's attention and everybody has settled down. "Let's start with News Ten, then we'll do the others." He pauses, hand on the remote to the cable box, while the two anchors at the station's news desk says good evening and exchange some dull remarks about the cold weather and the Syracuse basketball team. "They led with a death, as you might expect when there is one, and they have the setup of the scene, with the ambulance sitting idle while a gurney with the sheet draped over it is wheeled into its waiting back end. Here's what they say to describe the obvious and tease us into 'keeping it where it is.'" Gemma turns up the volume and lets the sound of the male anchor fill the room from a pair of speakers mounted on the wall. *"We have a sad story to report tonight, from out at Tanner Valley Golf course, where police say they have found the body of an older woman. Pamela, what can you tell us?"*

After the television camera focuses on a single sign, which defines the location as the Tanner Valley Golf Course, it then pans back to a blond woman, tousled hair moving in the night wind, holding a microphone. Angie, noticing that a crime scene investigation van and other police cars with lights flashing are also on the scene with the ambulance, feels the blood drain from her extremities. She stares open-mouthed at the reporter as she begins talking into the mic.

"That's right, Bob, there was indeed a body of an elderly female found out here on the slope of one of the fairways. Police didn't tell us just where the body was found, only that it appeared as if she may have been sledding. They said a sled was found near the deceased female, but it was unclear whether or not it was the deceased's sled, or one that was left there by someone else earlier."The reporter stamped her feet, steam rising from her breathing, looked back toward the assembled vehicles, and held up a gloved hand with a piece of paper in it as she indicated the presence of the uniformed people milling about. "Police have not yet released the name of the deceased. All we know now is they do not suspect foul play, but they are treating this as, at least, a very suspicious event. Back to you, Bob."

Bob shuffles some papers in the News Ten studio and looks up, knitting his brows, looking soulfully into the camera, and uttering in a deep voice, "Thanks, Pamela. We'll be following this story for you as it develops, here on News Ten."

Angie sits, stunned, mind racing while Professor Gemma asks the students what they thought of the newswriting style and content. She barely listens as she mulls over what she has just seen and heard. The rest of the class session passes by with her offering a minimum of input in her team discussion on the local stations' performances.

When class ends, Angie gathers her belongings with a hurried, distracted air and quickly turns to leave. Waiting just outside the classroom door, Jack leaves a small group of fellow students and falls alongside her. Swinging her backpack over her shoulder, she catches him with a glancing blow to his shoulder, a shot he uses as an opportunity to put her off guard.

"Hey, that thing is a deadly weapon," he opens. "You sure you're licensed to carry it?"

"Hey, Jack," says Angie, as she tries to contain a laugh. *He's too cute,* she thinks. Angie continues to slide past the other students and Jack follows closely behind.

"You taking off this early?"

"Yeah, I've got a crazy day. I need to finish my journalism ethics project, and there are a few things I need to research. Maybe I'll see you later, Jack."

"Hey, Ange, you're not still mad about last Friday night, are you?" he asks, sounding genuinely sincere.

Angie is confused for a second and puts her hand to the bridge of her nose.

"No, not at all. It's forgotten. But now that you bring it up, it was pretty stupid of you. I thought football practice was over. Running around Chuck's with me on your shoulders like a cheerleader was a little embarrassing. What, too much testosterone, too few outlets?"

"Yeah, you're right. Let's go back to that 'forgotten' part of what you just said," pleads Jack. "How about I walk with you?"

Angie smirks slightly and the corners of her lips curl upward. Jack takes note and relieves Angie of her backpack.

"What's in this? You taking up sculpture and have some boulders in here?"

"Physics is not only a heavy course, it needs heavy books," she says.

Like a guide through a mountain pass, Jack escorts Angie through the students going to and coming from classes. Bracing themselves in the foyer, Angie and Jack zip up their parkas and thrust themselves into the arctic air.

"Why didn't we go to a school in the South?" asks Angie.

"Because Syracuse has one of the best journalism departments in the country," says Jack.

"There are other pursuits."

"Good point. Where were you in my senior year in high school when I was looking at colleges?"

There is silence between them as they walk down the path toward their dorm. Other students stream past. It is too cold to expose their faces to the wind, never mind talk, so hand gestures take the place of words. Both Angie and Jack have their faces buried in the upright collars of their coats. Angie looks at Jack and then looks away. She repeats this routine a couple of times and Jack notices.

"What, you can't get enough of me?" he asks, mouth emerging from above his collar. It's a sarcastic tone he uses to mask an underlying hopefulness.

"You're not that cute. You kinda owe me a favor for what happened last week, right?"

"I thought we were going to forget about it, remember?"

Angie doesn't say anything, buries her face back into her coat, and pushes along. She reaches for her backpack on Jack's shoulder, but he refuses to relinquish it.

"I've got it." He looks at her. "All right, I was a little rowdy— too much Sammy Adams. So, I owe you one. What's up?"

Angie stops walking, pulls down her collar, and unravels her scarf from around her mouth. Jack spins back and drops the bag to his feet. The two of them are face to face, but the cold wind is unbearable, so they seek protection from behind a grove of evergreens off to the side.

"I really need a sympathetic ear and have nobody to talk to," says Angie. "My roommate is only focused on two types of sweets—one you eat with a fork and another that shaves."

"The guy from the bus?"

"Yeah, whatever. That's not the point. Remember when I was working on break, back at the newspaper, and I told you about that old guy dying on the sled at a golf course? Well, I think it just happened again."

"When did you go sledding?"

"I didn't. Are you listening? We just saw it in class. It was just like the one back at home. I'm wondering if I should go to the police or something," says Angie.

"And when you go to the police, what will you tell them? That you think these accidents are related?" asks Jack. Angie is quick with her response, and points her finger to make an emphatic point.

"That's just it. I don't think they are accidents! C'mon, Jack, don't you think it's kinda weird, too?"

"I think something similar happening to two older people in two separate incidents three hundred miles apart is more likely a coincidence. If there were the marks of Satan in the snow, that would point to a crime. I'm sure there will be something in the paper or on TV if it is anything," says Jack.

He takes Angie's scarf and gently wraps it around her face. Angie's arms lie limply at her sides as she stares at his smiling face. He pulls up her collar, and bends down for her backpack. "C'mon, I'll walk you to Physics." With a slight coax, he edges her onward, back on the path toward her next class.

CHAPTER 4

Care to Dance

Angie stretches her legs and leans back in her chair, which has broken support and makes a crackling noise from her movement. Staring vacantly at a large grease board covered in enigmatic symbols and bursts of letters and numbers seemingly stuck together randomly, she appears present in body if not entirely in mind. Her physics professor is talking, with the tightly controlled intensity of a television evangelist setting the stage before delivering the big message. "OK, people. Leonardo da Vinci. Ever hear of him? Hmm? How about Guillaume Amontons or Charles-Augustin de Coulomb?

Anybody? Anybody? What do you think they may discuss if they were all in the same room together? Hmm? Perhaps the Laws of Friction. The force of friction is directly proportional to the applied load, the force of friction is independent of the apparent area of contact, or kinetic friction is independent of the sliding velocity? Hmm? What do you think?"

Professor Karl Koogler is bouncing a basketball off the cement-block wall, lacking virtually any dexterity or coordination. He begins to roll the ball around, back and forth to the first row of sitting students, demonstrating the principles of friction. As the ball arrives back at his feet, he tries to flip it from his clunky, size-thirteen shoes as if he were actually a soccer star, not a nerdy professor.

This holds the attention of the students, not the subject matter. "Suppose a stone had a greater mass, hence a greater weight," Professor Koogler says, as he scribbles $g = constant$ on the board. The basketball is rolled back by one of the students and catches the professor by surprise, hitting the back of his leg. His voice is heightened and a bit shrilly. "The stone would then exert a greater force on the road, and more of the atoms of the road and the stone would be in contact," he continues. "Questions?"

The air is sucked out of the room as twenty-seven students collectively hope that no one is enough of a brown-nosing people pleaser to offer a question. *I'm positron I can't stand this anymore,* Angie puns to herself.

"Ms. Clarke? You look pensive. This make sense to you?"

Angie, embarrassed and subconsciously afraid her thoughts are somehow visible to this intimidating smart man, grabs a lock of her hair and turns it a few times before answering, "Yes, Mr. Koogler, I think I get it."

"Good! I love it when my students have a light go off in their head, even if it's moving so fast I can't measure it," he chuckles, pleased with himself. "Okay, see you Friday."

Feeling reprieved, Angie gets up quickly, avoiding eye contact with everyone so she won't have to hold up her end of a conversation. She slips past, down the aisle of the lecture hall, and makes her way outside. A weak, lemony sun has warmed things up slightly, but the wind still bites her face as she hurries back to Sadler Hall.

Back in her room, she fires up her Lenovo ThinkPad and hits her Google Chrome web browser icon. Going to her bookmarks, she clicks on the *Post-Standard* logo and then on Syracuse.com, the paper's website, and finds its obituaries. "Oh, my God,; here it is!" Scanning the highlights of the obit silently, she reads it with an increasing concern and wonderment.

Helen Thompson, eighty-five years old, beloved wife, mother, and grandmother, passed away yesterday. Funeral services will be at 8:15 a.m. Friday at Farone and Son Funeral Home, and at 9:00 a.m. at Blessed Sacrament Church, where a Mass of Christian burial will be celebrated. Burial will follow in Assumption Cemetery. Calling hours will be from 2:00 to 5:00 p.m. Thursday at the funeral home, 1500 Park Street, Syracuse. Condolences may be offered at Farone & Son Funeral Home, www.faroneandson.com. In lieu of flowers please make donations to FightSMA.com.

Angie pulls some strands of hair from the back of her head and starts to twirl. She picks up her iPhone, turns it on, and starts to scroll through her contacts. She begins to tap some numbers, then stops, thinking better of it, and puts the phone down. *Let's see—where do I start digging? Funeral the day after tomorrow. Maybe the best way to check this out would be to go to it. Make a list of relatives, see who shows and signs the guestbook. See if there's anyone she had in common with Mr. Fife, or someone in his family. Look up the Fife obit. Hmm, what else? Should I call Bill Armstrong? No, it'd be way cooler to just send him the story, like a pro's pro. Tie these all up with the who, what, when, where, and why. Follow up with the motive behind the motive. Serial killer who leaves a sled as a calling card? Weird—if that's it. But what else could it be? Could it be some cult like those people who all wore the same sneakers when they followed their leader to the Great Whatever?*

Angie spends the rest of the afternoon surfing the Web in her dorm room, eating some Trader Joe's melba toast squares with organic peanut butter, and some Pepperidge Farms Milano Melts she got in a care package from home. She washes down her steady graze of a meal with some seltzer water from her and Sarah's mini fridge, drinking from a Syracuse University beer mug. She tries website after website, Googling various combinations of keywords to find a reference to similar cases of older people dying on golf courses next to sleds. She switches to a search of news sites and checks out the LexisNexis website she subscribes to for her journalism classes. *I'm sure I saw a story about some old guy dying on a golf course out west somewhere,* she thinks over and over.

Barely aware that day has given way to dusk, Angie says, "I bet I'd get kicked out of a sorority for drinking a non-beer beverage out of this," before taking a sip of seltzer out of her mug, after licking peanut butter off a plastic knife.

"Well, you should at least be drinking something orange out of it, us being Orangemen and Orangewomen," says a voice by the door.

"How long have you been there, spy boy?" Angie asks, startled. She takes her glasses, which Sarah refers to as her "birth control" glasses, and puts them next to her laptop screen.

"Not long," Jack answers as he comes the rest of the way into Angie's room, and pulls a chair from Sarah's desk over to sit next to her. "My folks taught me it's not nice to eavesdrop on someone's private conversations. And conversation doesn't get any more private than one person talking to oneself."

"Jack, we're journalists. If we can't eavesdrop, we should lower our sights and settle for public relations."

"Good point, Scoop. You sound like a real journalist. Gotta eavesdrop if you wanna get ahead." Jack gets up and does a variant of the Funky Chicken dance.

Angie gapes at him with a look of mock horror. "What the heck is *that*?"

"It's the Funky Chicken, soul sister. My parents got a DVD collection of a show called *Soul Train* that they grew up with back in the seventies. I watched it with them over Thanksgiving. Other than the bright synthetic clothes that were too tight and too loose in the wrong places, the huge bird's-nest hairdos, and the garish makeup, they sure knew how to throw down back in the day."

"Jack, I am just so impressed with your cultural consciousness," Angie says. "If I ever get on some reality show and need a lifeline with an all-encompassing command of old-school mating dances, I'll keep you in mind."

"Wait until you see me do the Hustle."

They share a glance, enjoying the banter and each other's company. Angie breaks the moment, going for a lock of hair, then stopping herself. "Hey, you want to chase a story with me? I'm going to look into this death-near-a-sled thing and see where it goes. What do you say?"

Angie makes an absentminded grab for her glasses, reconsiders, and then returns them to her pocket. She pulls the obituary notice out from its saved spot on the dock at the side of her computer screen, and beckons Jack to look at it.

"Check it out—it adds up. This Helen Thompson woman was the same age as the guy from my hometown. There's something about this thing, I know it. You know about intuition, Jack? When you *know* something, you *know* it. And I can feel it here." She pounds a fist softly just beneath her sternum.

Jack doesn't say anything as he reads the obituary, then asks her to back up to the website where he can read the news story about the woman's death.

"So, what do you plan to do? Go to the police?"

Angie's shoulders sag.

"If I go the police, then they'll think I'm a nut. But I can't just sit on this thing; it will drive me crazy," she says. Jack's eyes lift upward, and his head nods in concurrence.

Angie begins to become more theatrical and starts to pace, and Jack simply watches.

"We'll go to the lady's funeral," she says, acting as if the idea had just occurred to her, seeking to draw him in by making him feel like part of the decision-making process. "Yes, that's it," says Angie in a tone of heightened excitement.

"Wait a minute. How did the pronouns get finalized here and the word *I* gets turned into *we*?"

Angie is no longer listening, deep into a hair-twirling event. "Okay, I'll swing by your room nine o'clock Friday. Make sure you're ready," she says. Angie looks at the obituary again. "Yeah, that's right. It's at ten o'clock a.m., so that should give us plenty of time. Make sure you dress nicely—no sweat pants." Angie gets up and says she has to get going to meet Sarah and some friends for dinner at the student union. "Hey, thanks, Jack. Breakfast is on me, OK?"

Jack gets up and waves ceremoniously, and, hoping to get the last word in, declares with as much assertiveness as he can muster, "And I'm getting the most expensive thing on the menu."

CHAPTER 5

Be-Cause

Angie spends Thursday bouncing from dorm to class to student union to class to dorm, thinking it an apt analogy for her internalized feeling of bouncing off the walls as she waits for Friday's funeral field trip. Getting back to her empty dorm room as the sun lowers behind the smallest of buildings, she decides to use her time researching her story instead of studying. Poring over the scant resources she has to connect the two deaths in the snow, she focuses on what she can learn from the Thompson obituary. Looking up the Fight SMA website and then several others on spinal muscular atrophy, she gets a quick education on a disease that she discovers hides in plain sight. Although it has a low profile, it is known to be one of the most prevalent genetic disorders.

Spinal muscular atrophy (SMA) is a motor neuron disease, affecting the spinal cord and brain stem. The motor neurons affect the voluntary muscles that are used for activities such as crawling, walking, head and neck control, and swallowing. It is a relatively common "rare disorder": approximately one in six thousand babies are affected, and about one in forty people are genetic carriers. SMA is the number one genetic killer of children under the age of two.

Angie closes her eyes and imagines what it would be like to fall apart from the inside out, as one of your most dependable structural components, your muscles, begin to fail. *Betrayed from within. I wonder if the Thompsons knew somebody with it, or what.* She reads on:

SMA affects muscles throughout the body, although the proximal muscles (those closest to the trunk of one's body, e.g., shoulders, hips, and back) are often most severely affected. Weakness in the legs is generally greater than in the arms. Sometimes feeding and swallowing can be affected. Involvement of respiratory muscles (muscles involved in breathing and coughing) can lead to an increased tendency for pneumonia and other lung problems. Sensation and the ability to feel are not affected. Intellectual activity is normal and it is often observed that patients with SMA are unusually bright and sociable. Patients are generally grouped into one of four categories, based on certain key motor function milestones.

SMA is an autosomal recessive genetic disease. In order for a child to be affected by SMA, both parents must be carriers of the abnormal gene, and both must pass this gene on to their child. Although both parents are carriers, the likelihood of a child inheriting the disorder is 25 percent, or one in four.

She stops reading, gets up, crosses the room, and goes to her bed. Lying on her stomach, she takes one of her pillows and hugs it to her chest, turning her head sideways on the other pillow. Face to face with her stuffed bear, Peter Panda, nubs worn smooth by a childhood of hands-on loving, she tries to absorb what she has been reading. To get a handle on the feeling, she tries to emotionally climb inside the possible range of feelings. *What is it like for those parents, in the solitude of their home, crying in each other's arms at the thought their love passed this gene to their child? Are they able to fathom why their child was stricken with SMA? Is it meaningful on a larger scale, beyond their immediate family? From where or from whom would they get the strength?*

Angie is snapped from her daydream by the unlocking and opening of her dorm room door, and a cackling laugh cuts through her contemplative mood like a rock through a plate-glass window. "Haha, you go, girlfriend. Pretending that pillow is Jack the Snack? Caught ya hugging, like a mugging!" Sarah sweeps in, all glitter and bluster, a slipstream of cold air attending to her like a bridesmaid to a bride. She kicks the door shut with the back of her foot. Paper snowflake cutouts and the girls' nameplates on the door shake with the reverberation. Sarah drops her books with a *clomp* on her desk, does an exaggerated bunny hop across the room, and belly flops with a bedspring-rattling landing next to her roommate.

"Hi, Sarah," says a still subdued Angie.

"Hiya, roomie! Hey, why the long face? Doin' your horse imitation? Put that with your birth-control glasses, you'll be single for stinkin' ev-ah!"

"Sarah, a reporter's life just may be better suited to someone single. The real good ones are better at watching other people live their lives."

"Ya mean bein' a wallflower is more like it, Ange." Sarah gestures with her head at a poster of Coldplay's Chris Martin over on her side of the room and blows it a kiss. "Now there is a flower on the wall, girlfriend. I would surely give all this up," she says, turning over onto her side and sweeping her arm around their cluttered room, "for just one night with *that* man. Haaaaha!" She turns and slaps Angie on her butt.

"C'mon, Ange, lighten up. Life with me isn't that bad."

Angie laughs despite herself. She turns onto her side and faces Sarah, who has picked up a copy of *The New Yorker* off Angie's bedside table. "Yo, what do you get out of this high-brow stuff? I mean, where's the beef? At least in *People*, you get to look at a hottie or two."

"That's one of the places I'd like to write for someday, Sar. It's one of the top magazines for breaking stories and good writing." Angie pauses and smiles. "But more importantly, you found a timely reference to food! I'm starved. I could really go for a big old cheeseburger covered with everything. What do you say we go off the reservation and get us a pitcher and some grilled animal tissue?"

"Eww. Put it like that, I just might consider going vegan," Sarah says, making a face. "But not tonight. Tonight, let there be beef! And after that, more beer!"

"Faegan's?" asks Angie.

"Faegan's," answers Sarah. "Where Hump Day Thursday is the new Friday!"

Angie gets up to join her waiting friend. *Note to self,* Angie thinks. *Have fun. This will all change when you graduate.*

They are just about out the door when her cell phone, set to vibrate so she could study in peace, begins to buzz, a fly caught between windowpanes. Taking it out, Angie sees someone left a text and hits the message app to look at it. *GKTW,* it says. "That's weird," says Angie, more to herself than to Sarah.

"What's weird?" her roommate asks.

"The message says 'GKTW,' but there's no return number."

"Maybe it's dreamboat Jack?" suggests Sarah.

"No, there's no number," says Angie. "I never heard of it before. It's short for some saying or something. Oh, well, no use worrying about it now. I'll remember to ask him about it later."

She won't remember.

CHAPTER 6

Arms Wide Open

Friday morning comes both too early and not soon enough for Angie. She takes longer than usual to get dressed, changing outfits, trying to find a happy medium between an appropriate mourning and investigative reportorial look. Settling on a gray business pantsuit her mother helped her pick out for job interviews and the like, she pauses, looking at herself in the mirror. Showing her unfamiliarity with makeup application, she puts on and quickly wipes off red lipstick before settling on cherry red

Chapstick, as a compromise to practicality and trying to look more grown up.

"Girlfriend, watching you put on makeup is like watching a duck put on ballet shoes," says a groggy voice from across the room. Sarah, just the top of her tousled head poking out from under a pile of bedclothes, says, "You want to stand out or fit in?"

"Uh, fit in, sorta. Sorry if I woke you."

"Well, you want to be noticed by your friend, keep your glasses in your bag, skip the makeup, and let him see you for who you are. He's not the flashy type, and you got a keeper. So, be a keeper. Beekeeper! Get it?"

"Sarah, you are really one of a kind." Angie laughs. "Why don't you let people see this part of you more often?"

"I'll try, Ange, I'll try."

"Okay, Sar, go back to sleep. I'll see you later. Your turn to take notes in Physics, 'kay?"

"You got it, roomie. May the Schwartz be with you!"

Rolling her eyes, Angie takes a final look at herself in the mirror, shoots a peace sign at Sarah, says good-bye and leaves the room, shutting the door softly.

Self-conscious about the clacking of her heels as she walks down the empty hallway, Angie looks at her watch, realizing she is running late to pick up Jack and head to the funeral. Scurrying down the stairs to his dorm room, she realizes she is also out of practice wearing anything but clogs and sneakers, and nearly stumbles as she pivots on a landing.

"Actuarial tables show us that we will fall on a stairway once every twenty-two hundred times," a voice says from just beneath her. She stops. Jack, in a blue blazer, red tie, white shirt, and charcoal pants, moves to greet her at the bottom of the stairs. "And once for every seven hundred thirty-four thousand times you use a stairway, you will suffer a painful fall that will require care at a hospital."

"Jack, other than knowing better than to scare someone this early in the morning, how the heck do you know such obscure facts about stairway accidents?"

"When your father owns his father's insurance company that he inherited from his father, you learn actuarial tables pretty much by osmosis," Jack says as he offers a chaste hug to Angie. "And you learn if you don't want to be in the family insurance business for the rest of your life, you'd better learn your way out of it by working in it during the summers, so you can earn your way out of it with a good old Syracuse education."

"Well, did you know that according to the laws of physics, of which there happens to be plenty, the mechanics of motion would indicate that a descent down a stairway is nothing more than a controlled act of falling?"

"I did not know that, Ange. Wow."

"Then I guess you don't really know jack, do you, Jack?"

They look at each other for a minute, seeing each other dressed as grown people. Both grin and nod with an unaffected, honest appreciation.

"Enough banter; we got to canter," Angie says, breaking off the mutual admiration. "Let's get on our horse and ride."

They walk from their dorm to the Sadler parking lot, carrying on their conversation to keep warm, as well as to keep their connection alive.

"You ready for this, Jack?" Angie asks.

"You bet, Ange, but it's your lead. I'm just here to learn from an already accomplished reporter. Me, I got football to fall back on."

"One summer doesn't make me Brian Williams," says Angie. "And as far as you go, a good football player doesn't actually 'fall.' You may have been a star in high school, but you're still pretty small-time in the ACC. I mean, it took you four years to make third string. I'd concentrate on your news skills."

"Right. So, if I don't have news-gathering street cred, and I don't have football skills for the NFL, I do have my superhero good looks. I can be"—he affects a deep, melodramatic tone—"Anchorman!"

Angie laughs, punches him playfully on the shoulder, and says: "You're not *that* good-looking."

Arriving at her old clunker, Angie struggles to force the key into a water-frozen lock, finally succeeds, and shoots him a glance over the hood. "No remarks about the mess in here, and no wisecracks about the way this baby runs. Bell, she's a beautiful thing."

"Angie, all I can say is this car ought to be allowed to RIP." He smiles. "Rust in peace."

"Funny man, you may be an anchorman after all. How about a weatherman, or a sportscaster, even?" she mutters as she pops the passenger side door for Jack. She turns on her iPhone's navigation app and sets it in a cup holder. Traffic is relatively light, and they reach the church in what seems like no time to the nervous pair of novice reporters. A gauzy light shines through an icy mist, which is punctuated softly by the glimmering of taillights as they pull up to the church parking lot. Many of the mourners have arrived at the same time, and doors open to let people out as if the whole affair has been carefully choreographed. Angie decides to park on the street adjacent to the parking lot along the side of the church, and the car coughs before shuddering to a stop. Jack just looks at Angie, who is holding up one finger as if to silence him. An older couple glances their way.

As they walk up the long, granite stairs leading to the church, Angie tries to get a read on who's who among the crowd. On the exterior, they all look pretty much the same, she thinks, dressed in dark clothing and appropriately somber. She finds herself wondering who knew Helen Thompson in what capacity, who was special to her or her to them. The stairs narrow into a single file as they enter the church through a large mahogany door. Angie and Jack let a couple of people who have entered from the side cut in line. One is a young girl, about eight years old, in a wheelchair. A black man who looks to be about forty years old is pushing her.

The girl looks at them briefly with a glimmer of curiosity, then faces forward again as the man wheeling her chair leans close to her and says softly, "Here we go, Steph. We have a pathway." The man has strong chiseled features and an athletic build. He looks to be six feet, perhaps a shade more, wearing a navy blue suit with a white shirt and light blue tie. His face is open and friendly, exuding confidence. He has that elusive thing referred to as charisma. Angie is absorbed by the two. *Maybe she's a niece or a granddaughter of Helen Thompson. I bet the man with her is her caregiver.*

"Hey, what are you doing?" whispers Jack, watching her drift toward the front. "Let's sit over here." Jack guides Angie to a back corner aisle seat. The words to "Ave Maria" float down from the choir above. The soloist's voice is angelic, and the accompanying organist plays with solemnity interspersed with theatrical flourishes. The church is large and it feels intimidating to Angie. Dark wooden pews with hand-carved armrests and the Stations of the Cross run in a straight line from the front to back along the center aisle. There are smaller aisles to the left and right, but the main center aisle is where all the activity is designed to take center stage. A couple of priests and two altar boys begin making their way from the altar toward the back of the church. One of the priests, a small roundish man, is dressed more formally than the other, appearing to be the one in charge. One of the altar boys looks to be about sixteen and the smaller boy appears to be ten years old. The older, more confident boy guides the younger one as they carry out the liturgical tasks. It is quiet enough that even those sitting in the remote area of the church can hear the turning pages of the priest's large book.

"I haven't been to one of these since I was a little girl," Angie, says, tone hushed, into Jack's ear.

Angie's heart rate quickens and her lips turn dry. She grabs a section of hair and begins to twirl it, around and around. Sensing her anxiety, Jack reaches over to hold her hand and she lets hers fall into his. The heavy mahogany doors, decorated with ornate carving, open and the pallbearers, all of whom are middle-aged or younger, begin to escort the casket into the church. The casket stops short of where the priests are standing, and the older altar boy hands the main celebrant the incense, which is rocked back and forth and around the casket.

The chain from the incense canister clangs ceremoniously as the priests recite their prayers in unison, welcoming the casket. The strong smell of incense permeates the still air. Angie crinkles her nose and sneezes loudly. She looks around and notices the wheelchair-bound girl's caregiver, who is looking in her direction. The smoke residue and aroma rise to the sculpted figures of the church's ceiling. After a brief prayer by the main celebrant, the procession slowly moves down the long aisle to the front of the altar.

"Look at all these people," Angie says into Jack's ear. "What a great turnout for her. There's so much accumulated love here. That's what a great life must add up to, don't you think?"

Jack simply nods in agreement.

"I'm kind of sorry we came," Angie continues. "I feel sort of ashamed, almost guilty, like we did something wrong, that we're invading their privacy. You know what I mean?"

"There you go again with the word *we*. I was perfectly content to stay on campus and go to class. This was all your idea, remember?" Jack whispers back.

"Shush," says Angie.

The roundish priest announces that Helen Thompson's eldest son, William, will say a few words about his mother. William walks up to the lectern and adjusts the microphone so it is positioned in front of his mouth. He reaches into the side pocket of his jacket and removes a piece of paper that he slowly unfolds. The microphone picks up every sonic nuance of the rustling paper. His eyes rise to meet the stares of the congregation, he takes a deep swallow, and coughs once into a folded hand.

"Excuse me," he says. "Good morning. What a wonderful tribute to my mother and family to have you all here with us today. My mom would be partially embarrassed by all this support. I want to take a brief moment to thank you for all your support over this last week. You all mean the world to me and my family."

He pauses, and coughs again. "You know, my mom taught us life lessons seamlessly. She taught leadership, by allowing us to be leaders. She taught communication, not by speaking, but by always listening. She taught confidence by making us feel wonderful and safe. She taught humility by making us aware of fragility. She taught motivation by her gratitude and selflessness. She taught us that a soft approach is a strong approach. She taught us that a person's actions can speak louder than one's words. She taught honesty will gain trust and integrity. She taught us compassion by teaching us to look into and through the eyes of the less fortunate. She taught us love by always putting others first.

"We just spent Thanksgiving with my mom a few weeks ago and like always, it was wonderful, and we'll always have wonderful memories to cherish. Thanksgiving was a special time in our family, but for me, the smells that remind us of giving and caring are not of candied yams coming out of the oven, or a large bird sitting on the counter to cool before carving. Instead, it is the smell of the hall in the basement of this church, one level below us. It was my mom's tradition, a tradition that we'll continue. We'll serve food to the homeless on Thanksgiving morning. My mom taught us how to fulfill ourselves, not with consuming, but with giving. But that was who she was—a teacher, a giver."

Angie can't stop her eyes from filling, and can't put the brakes on her emotions as a few tears wind their way down her cheek. Jack, looking over at her, gives her a scrunched-up Kleenex that has probably spent the better part of four seasons in his jacket.

William lightens the mood with a funny story about how his mother once tricked him with one of her impersonations. "Mom made sure we all practiced what she would have us preach when it came to helping others. One day midweek about twenty years ago, I was visiting a customer and needed to use a pay phone. This was pre-cell phone days, if you can remember back then. Anyway, I'm not sure how she knew I would be in the vicinity, but she made a point of having us cross paths on this fateful day. I was on the pay phone outside the grocery store, and saw this elderly woman having trouble carrying multiple grocery bags across the parking lot. It was at least eighty degrees and she was wearing a winter coat, struggling, stopping and starting along the way. As I was on the phone, I witnessed people driving around her, trying to navigate for a parking space, or others not offering to help. Each time she stopped, it seemed harder to get started again. Anyway, long story short, I ran up to her and offered to help her, get a taxi or something. She refused, so I offered to drive her home. After some negotiating, she said OK and we began the drive. She seemed to have dementia, because we drove around town for forty-five minutes until she had me pull down her street. This is my mom's street, I thought. Then she had me stop in front of her house. She pulled off her wig and glasses, bent over, and kissed me. 'I'm so proud of you,' she said and laughed. I'll never forget that day. She was unbelievable."

Nods of familiarity and smiles of recognition are passed among the congregation as William tells this and several other stories about his mom's quirks, foibles, and habits. Then he pauses again and gets serious once more.

"And you know there was a weight on my mother's shoulders. We all know what that weight was, the weight of a physical disability. She watched a little girl—one so dear to her that she probably set her own heartbeat to the beat of that little girl's heart—suffer to do the smallest, most basic movements other children do easily as soon as they are able. The move-ments like standing up for the first time and grasping out for her mommy's hand. Like walking across a room to pick out her favorite dolly, and hold it close to her while she cuddles with her grandmother on a couch by a roaring fireplace."

Several throats clear in the audience as William pauses. "Well, a love like that can go one of several ways. One is to feel so sorry for the little girl that she tries to do every-thing she can—in a physical sense—to make sure the girl gets what she wants delivered to her." He pauses and looks at his daughter, Steph. "Another way is to help that little girl learn the limitations of the body are not limitations of the mind, that limits are more often self-imposed than they are real. That kind of love helps a little girl push against limits until the lines set by those limitations begin to blur and eventually dissolve. And when limitations dissolve, that's when a poor little girl everyone feels sorry for and pities can become what she is supposed to be, which is simply 'a little girl,' not a 'poor little girl.' That, my friends and family, is what my mom, Helen Thompson, did. She helped make Steph become a little girl. That is the kind of love my mom had. That is how strong her love was."

As William steps around the lectern and walks back to his pew at the front of the church, there are a few audible sniffles and the honking of noses.

"She must have been a special lady," says Angie softly. Because Jack has nothing else to offer, Angie beings searching in her handbag for another tissue, unsure exactly why she is so moved by the sentiments of strangers, and somewhat embarrassed at feeling like an interloper. "She reminds me so much of my grandmother, Jack."

"I guess, but I don't think there is anything unusual here, Ange. What do you say we leave, and let this family have their privacy, huh?" says Jack quietly.

"Agreed."

Angie and Jack quietly leave the church, only to find their car is blocked, forcing them into waiting for the service to end. The immediate family is the first out the door. Angie and Jack sit in their car and watch the casket being borne down the granite stairs. Salt pellets crunch under the shoes of the mourners. Angie sees the granddaughter again as she and her caregiver exit through the side door, where there is a concrete ramp.

"Look at that adorable girl. My heart aches when I see that," she says.

"Yeah, I know what you mean," responds Jack. Angie's eyes are fixed on the couple and it's not until Jack taps a drumbeat on the Honda's dash that Angie snaps back to the present. "What do you say, Ange, ready to take me for a king's breakfast?"

"Just as long as you don't make me vomit," she shoots back at him, trying to sound funny, tough and unaffected by their shared experience of captured intimacy.

Angie starts the car, but then sits back and slumps in her seat, looking out her side window as the girl, Steph, is wheeled toward a white, Chevy minivan. Angie and the caregiver make eye contact as they pass by. His eyes seem to fix on Angie's. Angie looks around to see if she is mistaken.

"What's up?" asks Jack. Angie looks left and right again, and back at the caregiver through the side mirror. "Hey, Ange, what are you doing?"

"In a sec, Jack, in a sec," says Angie, brushing him off.

Angie touches the window-down button on the side of her door, and turns slowly around to look over her left shoulder. Steph looks at her caregiver and they simultaneously smile at each other. Then they both look directly at Angie, using their right hands to make a gesture. Raising their hands to their right eyes, they tap their right index fingers to their right thumbs twice, while simultaneously winking their right eyes.

At that same instant, Angie's foot slips off the clutch, and the car lurches forward until her foot finds the brake again and slams it home—hard. Angie and Jack's heads snap forward, a mini whiplash.

"What. The. Heck. Are you doing?" yells Jack.

"I'm sorry, I'm sorry," says Angie. She turns around again to look back at Steph and the caretaker, eschewing the mirror this time. Steph is just about situated in the backseat now, and her caretaker walks around the front of his van, without making further eye contact with Angie. He starts the van and, guided by the team of funeral directors, joins the procession to the cemetery. Angie restarts her car, stomps on the clutch, and lunges the stick shift into first gear.

"We're going!" she says loudly, gripping the steering wheel tightly with her left hand.

"Yeah, off to a king's breakfast," says Jack with a smile.

"Not so fast, Jabba the Hutt. We're going to the cemetery first!"

Angie jets out and cuts off another car in the procession. She throws her arm out the window in an apologetic manner.

"Angie Clarke…what are you doing…have you gone mad?" asks Jack in a strong tone. Angie pretends to be focusing on the traffic and where she is going. Jack unbuckles his seatbelt and the interior car alarm sounds. "Tell me what's up, or I am out of here, right now!"

"They *winked* and did this hand thingy at me!"

"Hand thingy?"

"Yeah. I don't know what it is called or what it means, but it was definitely something directed to me. That, I am sure of."

Jack raises his hands in confusion and looks out his window, as if to seek the opinion of a stranger.

"Well, when you put it that way, then it totally makes sense," he says sarcastically. Jack pauses for a second and looks at her. "Ange, I think you have officially snapped."

"Okay, okay, I've snapped. We're here anyway. Just a few more minutes, and you can even order bacon and sausage," she says impatiently. "Eat a whole pig if you want to."

"I think you've seen one too many movies, if you ask me," replies Jack.

"I haven't," Angie snaps. She parks the car up on the hill and looks down at the family members as they start to assemble around the gravesite. The cold mist has stopped, but it feels like the temperature has plummeted ten more degrees. Steph's caretaker is by her side, kneeling on one knee so they can see each other's faces. The priest from the church stands in front of the casket, and starts reciting a prayer from a small black book while flipping through an array of ribbon placeholders. Angie and Jack can't hear his exact words but can see the puffs of steam coming from his mouth. As he completes the final prayer, members of the family carefully walk across the frozen ground toward the casket to say their final goodbyes. Fearful of slipping, the women are escorted by the men. Steph's parents lay a rose on the casket, console each other, and slowly walk back to the lead car.

As the rest of the contingent files back into their cars, Steph's caregiver, in a seemingly private moment, scoops up some loose snow and forms it into a ball. He raises it to Steph's lips and she proceeds to kiss it. The caregiver then takes off one of his gloves and etches something on its surface with his right index finger, and lays it elegantly on the casket. He looks skyward, closes his eyes, and raises his outwardly stretched arms to the heavens. Angie and Jack are frozen in position.

"A little dramatic, don't you think?" asks Jack.

Still motionless, Angie continues to stare and ignores Jack. Jack shrugs his shoulders and walks back to the car. For a second, she watches where he is going as he mumbles to himself. Then she refocuses on Steph and the caregiver. By this time, Steph is back in the van and the caregiver is walking in front of it. He stops, looks up the hill to Angie, and nods. Angie acknowledges his visual contact and nods back to him. The caregiver eases himself into the van and it departs, following the red lights heading off in the distance. Angie is alone.

She looks back at Jack, who is now sitting in the car. The windows have fogged a little and he wipes away the condensation to keep Angie in view. Angie looks back down toward the casket and then back at Jack. She turns toward the casket and slowly takes her first step down the embankment. There is dead silence, except for the creaking noise that comes from the car door as Jack opens it.

"Are you kidding me?" comments Jack in a loud whisper. Angie continues her slow descent, ignoring Jack, who steps out and slams the door with all his might. The ice that has formed around the front fender breaks and falls to the ground. "Damn it!" he says, as he turns to kick the front tire.

By this point, Angie is no longer in view, so Jack stretches his neck and proceeds to walk toward the edge of the slope where she once stood. Just as Angie approaches the flat section, she slips and falls on her back, and lets out a stifled cry. She slides only a few feet and is quick to get up and brush off the remnants of snow. Angie looks around to see if anyone has noticed her covert operation, as if her mission is now compromised by her fall. She looks up the hill to see Jack. Likewise, he looks around to see if anyone has been watching her. From his vantage point, Jack can see in the distance that the workers are starting to gather around a tractor and backhoe.

"Damn it, Angie. What are you doing?" he says to himself.

Angie stops. She looks up to Jack for guidance and he motions for her to retreat. She ignores his request and quickens her pace to her target. Angie can now see the backhoe coming her way, so she lengthens her stride to a run. Her eyes begin to tear but she refuses to blink, afraid that she'll lose her focus on the snowball. Finally, she starts to decipher the inscription, when the rumble from the tractor sends a vibration across the stiff ground. Angie looks toward the tractor and then quickly focuses back on the snowball, only to watch it slide from its place of rest and fall to the ground, coming apart.

"Nooo!" she yells.

Seeing the look of disappointment in Angie's face, the operator of the tractor pulls back on his lever and brings his machine to a sudden halt. The front of the tractor swings a little from its abrupt stop and forward momentum. The operator reaches out with his hands for the others to stop as well. Dejected, Angie's head swings low and she slowly proceeds to walk up the winding path to where her car is parked.

CHAPTER 7

Frost Heaves

Driving I-90 across the relatively lightly traveled expanse of New York and Massachusetts toward Arlington, Angie has plenty of time to think about how she is going to tell her parents she has left school for possibly a week to follow a story. The insistent, low buzzing of her beat-up but beloved Honda's aging exhaust system offers counterpoint to her worried thoughts. *What if I'm just wasting my time?* she wonders over and over. *How do I explain I have to follow a hunch and it turns out that's all it is, a hunch? My parents have worked hard to send me to college and I'm blowing off*

a week on a whim. They are definitely going to ask about my classes. Her thoughts cycle back and forth, through guilt at leaving school and thinking she needs to concentrate on her story. *But I know I'm on to something. Trust your gut, Dad would say. So maybe they won't be that upset. Yeah, right.*

The hubs of Albany and Springfield provide the only thickening points of traffic to disturb her fantasies until she nears the exit for I-95, which she takes then jumps off of after a few miles to get onto Route 2 East for the last leg of her trip home. She decides to fire up her iPod. The contraption, retrofitted to use the car radio via a wire snaking into a power converter plugged into the lighter, reminds her of an intubation device. The song "How to Save a Life" by The Fray fills up the car as she sings along, slightly off-key but full of the song's emotion. She's halfway through a Dunkin' Donuts Extra-Extra coffee.

Angie gets off at the final exit, and heads down the familiar and almost ironically named Pleasant Street before turning right onto Gould Road. Near the end of the road, she pulls up to the Queen Anne-style house where she grew up. She parks the car and gets out, looking down the road toward Spy Pond. *Frozen over and covered with snow a few weeks from Christmas is not something that happens every year*, she notes to herself, wondering if it will get cleared off and be ready for some impromptu neighborhood hockey games. *All the young kids will pretend to be Tyler Seguin, or Milan Lucic, while the old-schoolers will bring their Bobby Orr game to the pond.*

She looks across the street at one house to the left, and a familiar pang of sadness, beyond words she has ever been able to articulate, strikes her without warning, as it often does when she hasn't prepared herself for the memory of who lived there. An old metal swing set, looking derelict through years of neglect, sits idle and forlorn in a side yard grown unkempt and a house gone partway to seed. *I remember swinging on that when it was new and painted red. That was about the only red redder than Marcie's hair. When she still had hair.*

Her musings are interrupted by the metallic squawk of the storm door opening at the front of her house. Cliff Clarke, a reasonably fit fifty-four-year-old stands at the top of the low stoop leading into their house, smiling at his daughter, a look of mild surprise on his face. "Hey there, Angie, what's cookin'? This is a surprise. Your mom is going to be ecstatic. Here for a short weekend?" At six foot one, Cliff looks like he visits the gym and enjoys playing the role of a weekend athlete.

"Uh, no, Dad. I mean, yes. I just needed to get away for a bit."

"Great, get in here before I pay for heating the street. I'll get your bags." He holds the door for his daughter as she shuffles in, head down, a little embarrassed, obviously uneasy.

Angie walks through the hall and into the living room, her family's distinctive smell filling her nostrils with warmth, and the accustomed layout of the room comforting her eyes after the monotony of watching the road roll by.

Cliff comes into the house, closing the door, and sets her bags down. "Hmmm. About twenty pounds in the duffel, your computer, and no book bag," he says, looking at her over the top of his reading glasses. "Definitely not an overnighter. The calendar says still seventeen shopping days 'til Christmas, which means there are still some lectures to go until finals. So, amateur sleuth that I am tells me that something isn't right in Kansas. You have something you want to tell me, I think. So, Angie, what's up?"

"Well, yeah, but how about we grab a soda and camp out in the kitchen for few seconds first? When will Mom be home?"

"Shortly. This is her Saturday on at the library. Hey, you're not sick or anything? You okay?"

"Oh, yeah, Dad. I'm fine."

Cliff and Angie go their separate ways. Angie hits the bathroom first and then rejoins her dad, who is sitting at the kitchen table, watching the head on a freshly poured Guinness settle into a state of perfection.

"Dad, remember that man, Charlie Fife, Sr., who died at the Winchester Golf Course?"

"Yes, of course I remember. Charlie was famous here before I was famous." He smiles. "I remember hearing from just about everyone who was there, about Old Charlie running for sixty-two yards in the frozen mud, with less than a minute on the clock against Somerville High. Definitely an Arlington High Spy Ponder legend, and probably only second in name recognition to Coach Eddy Burns. You did a story on him dying around Thanksgiving. And…?"

"Dad," says Angie, leaning against the center island. "Listen to this. There was a woman up at school, same age as Mr. Fife, and she died. Get this—froze to death on a golf course in the snow. And, *and* she was found dead the same way—next to a sled. She'd been sledding out in the snow, alone at night, just like Mr. Fife. And she died." Words rush out now like a steep mountain stream after a spring snowmelt. "Dad, something's going on. I *know* something's going on. I know it. So far, no one else is putting the two together, and I think there may be even more because I remember seeing something just like it on the Internet. Anyway, I saw something at the funeral that may be related. A little girl in a wheelchair who was just so adorable. Adorable and sad, not entirely sad, but definitely just *filled* with this wisdom. You could see it in her eyes. And the guy wheeling her, he…"

"Whoa, hold on, Angie. Let me get caught up here. Two elderly people died sledding instead of golfing, and you think maybe a young lady pushed in a wheelchair by some man who is traveling around the Northeast could be mixed up in the death of these people? Like a homicide or something?" Cliff sits next to Angie on the couch and cocks his head at her. "I think I need a little more information."

"It could also be Montana, but that was from a blog that I'm trying to find."

"What?"

"Well, I don't have a lot more specifics, Dad, but I'm serious. This is the kind of thing that comes along and you have to take it. Jack—you remember Jack from Homecoming, right? Jack went to the funeral with me, and pretty much agrees that something is happening here, and it could be huge."

"How is Jack? Nice guy. You two serious or something? He'd be a good sportscaster or weatherman, I'd bet."

"Dad, stop. We aren't even really 'not serious' yet, so relax with your football-playing, son-in-law fantasy league, okay? Besides, this isn't about Jack. It's about a story that I have discovered and I have to, *have* to follow it wherever it goes. It's the reporter in me, Dad."

Cliff watches his daughter intently. "Okay, let's say you *do* take some time off to do this. What about your classes?"

"I'm only going to miss one class if I get back by Wednesday, and Sarah is going to take notes for me. I haven't missed a class yet this semester, and you get two unexcused absences, anyway." She looks at her father expectantly. She's twirling her hair, winding strands up above her ear, and then letting them unwind. "Dad, you know I wouldn't be doing this if I wasn't sure. Have I ever just done something impulsively?"

"You mean other than trying to jump the picnic table with your Huffy bike and creating your own neighborhood X-Games tournament in our backyard? I think we took three kids from the neighborhood to Lahey Clinic for stitches, sprains, and a fracture that afternoon."

"I've thought about this. For one thing, I'm going to talk to Mr. Armstrong over at the paper. I know I'll get farther if I have the *Advocate*'s backing. He'll have some way to make sure I'm covered." She waits a few seconds, impatience conquering restraint.

"Well, honey. I learned a long time ago—well, maybe not that long ago—but several years into parenthood that I wasn't helping you become everything you could be by monitoring every little movement and activity you were about to undertake, just because my parents did that with me. It eventually dawned on me that fear keeps a father from being a good one."

"Does that mean I have your blessing to do this?"

"It means I will help you convince your mother that we ought to let you do this. She believes it's her job to rein you in, just like I think it's my job to let you run. Sound like a deal?"

"Yay, Dad!" She throws her arms around her father and kisses him on his cheek.

CHAPTER 8

Swing Oil

U pstairs, Angie finds her room just like she left it after Thanksgiving, aside from a small pile of clean clothes that just needs to be put in the proper drawers. Her bed is made, powder blue bedspread with an L.L. Bean purple down comforter folded at its foot. Photos of Angie holding a tennis racquet, carrying an oversized hockey bag, and smiling a gap-toothed smile as a ten-year- old wearing a tutu are set on her bureau, along with a wealth of trophies depicting female athletes in various stages of performance. There is a medium-sized mirror set in a tilting frame atop an antique green bureau.

And there it is. To a stranger visiting Angie's room, it would just be what it is—a hairbrush. Pink with black bristles, it has a diamond-shaped handle tapered at the end. It sits just to the side of the mirror, and to Angie, it might as well be lit with Christmas lights and beeping like a smoke detector. For her, the hairbrush is a cherished memento and a link to her first best friend, her first real attachment to someone other than her immediate family. To Marcie.

It wasn't until many years after Marcie died that Angie was able to grasp intellectually how Marcie came to die. She was never able to grasp *why* she died. It was shortly after her fifth birthday that the first signs of what was stalking Marcie, an invasive force made up of malignant white blood cells, began to appear. Kindred spirits, the two of them spent hours baking pretend cakes in their Hasbro Easy Bake Ovens, dressing up their Barbies, and swinging on the swings in Marcie's side yard.

While the swing set, which went unused for the last year of Marcie's life, serves as a savage mockery of Marcie's all-too-short life, the hairbrush offers an opposite perspective of her friend, a fond symbol of remembrance. During that last year of Marcie's life, when her curly red hair began to fall off, first in strands, then in clumps until there was nothing left,

Marcie used to brush Angie's hair for hours and hours. At first, Angie felt a child's undefined guilt that she had hair and Marcie did not. When she blurted out one day as she looked at her friend, eyes appearing to have grown huge in her face without the balance of cascading curls to frame them, that she was going to cut her hair off, too, Marcie looked at her in a way Angie never forgot.

"No! Please don't do that," Marcie said, her face so serious it appeared to belong to one far beyond her years. "Then we'll both look silly. Besides, I really like brushing hair. Maybe you can let me brush your hair since I don't have any."

And so she did. For hours and hours, while Marcie rested up from the debilitating rounds of chemotherapy and radiation she had to undertake, in an effort to win her life back from the invasive force running through her that was trying to wrest it away. Later, Angie was able to put a formal, more impartial name to that force—acute lymphoblastic leukemia. But at the time, the fact something could steal her friend away from Angie while she was in plain sight was incomprehensible. The moments she spent over at Marcie's house, while her friend brushed her hair, talked about dolls, and Angie told her about kindergarten, were intensely sad, but they were the moments they had, and therefore they were invaluable to Angie.

Angie picks up the hairbrush and cradles it bristles up in her palm, looking into it as if there were something buried in it, some secret to be revealed, and only she could break it down to its atoms and decipher it. A key as to why some children suffer so horribly and others live, only to have to watch and suffer along with them. As Angie turns the brush over in her hands, her mother, Sue, knocks in announcement of her presence at the partially opened door.

"Hi, sweetie. Dad says you've decided to spend a few days at home. Everything all right?"

"Hi, Mom. Everything's fine. He tell you why I'm here?"

They embrace and Sue guides some of her daughter's hair away from her face.

"Yeah, he did. He said you are following up a story you started for the *Advocate*. Is that—"

Angie cuts her off, almost absently, an act devoid of rudeness. "Mom, what do you remember about Marcie?"

Sue notices that Angie is holding Marcie's childhood hairbrush, so she moves toward the end of the bed, sitting on the right side, providing ample space if Angie decides to join her. "Oh, gee, honey. That was such a long time ago. You were so little and it all happened so fast. All of us, the Johnsons maybe most of all, were so surprised when such a healthy child got so sick so fast and…"

"Yeah, I know, Mom. I know it was fast. But did we ever find out why it happened? Was there something that ran in her family, genetics? Was there something in the environment or something? Did they ever dig deep, you know, like an investigation or something?"

"Well, no, Angie. I don't think they ever did an investigation, and if there was something in the Johnson family background that would have caused it, we certainly never heard about it. And I don't recall hearing about a lot of other kids getting her kind of cancer, or any other kind, as a matter of fact. And I think I would have heard about it working in the children's library."

"Yeah, I know, but it's just that I still can't make sense of why it happened to such a great person, such a great kid, you know? And as I get older, I don't know—I guess it hits you differently. Like I feel different about it now than when I was in high school or when I was at Bracket Elementary."

"I know, Angie, I know. I think it's all about perspective and how that changes as you get older. The way you look at things can't help but change. Do you remember what you said right after we told you Marcie had died?"

"Not really. I just remember crying and not being able to stop. I remember running across the street and swinging on the swing for hours, refusing to come off, and how you and Dad brought me a coat and sat on the ground, watching me with a flashlight until I fell asleep. I just couldn't believe that I wouldn't see her again. It was raw pain. Kids are honest with how they feel."

"I remember your tears, too, honey. It was horrible to see you in such pain. But what I remember the most is what you asked us through those tears. You looked at me with those big eyes, shiny with so many, many tears, and you asked us, 'Why did God have to take *her*? I thought God was nice!' It was heartbreaking to hear such a little girl ask that question, to see our little girl with that much hurt in her. And it was such an impossible question to answer. It was then and it is now."

"I know, Mom. I've asked that question and come up short of answers. It seems like forever."

Listening at the door, Cliff tries to lighten the mood. "You two solving the problems of the world?"

"Not yet, but we're working on it, Daddy."

"That's my girl. 'Life serves you lemon, you make…' what?"

"Lemon chicken from Panda Express?"

"Anyway, we can talk about your story later," her mother says. Taking Angie's face in her hands, she says, "So how is my baby? You tired? Hungry? I hate you driving by yourself, you know. Come on, let me take a look at you." She steps back, looks into her daughter's eyes. "Ah, you sure are beautiful. You look great."

Slightly embarrassed, Angie tries to brush off the compliment. "Yeah, Mom, I know, but how are you guys doing? Where's Daisy?"

"She's good. I guess she's worn out, probably sleeping on the sun porch. She thinks she's a cat more than a dog these days. What do you say we go downstairs? You can go wake her up and we'll have an early-ish dinner and then we can get caught up."

"'Kay, Mom. Let me just wash up and I'll be right down."

After a quick shower and a switch into flannel pajamas and an oversized Syracuse sweatshirt she had borrowed one autumn weekend from Jack, Angie goes downstairs and finds her small Havanese asleep on her fleece dog bed in the now darkening sunroom.

Angie bends down and wrestles with her pal now edging toward old age, rubbing the dog's belly.

"There's my Daisy. How's my girl? Mom, how much are you feeding her? She's turning into a little piglet. Come on, ya piggly poo. How's my little sausage link?"

Sue makes a pot of tea while Angie lets Daisy out to perform her biological functions. Angie holds the door for Daisy, who tends to her business, poised tail up daintily next to a hydrangea, before sprinting excitedly into the house.

"Pee and poop?" asks Sue.

"Uh, yeah, she dropped the deuce, Mom, if you really need to know."

"Deuce?" questions Sue, as she tilts her head in confusion.

"Poop, Mom," says Angie, as she holds up two fingers. Sue cracks a sheepish grin, grabs a dog treat from a box in the pantry, and gives it to Daisy. Daisy takes the treat and runs off to her bed, trying to bury it under her pillow.

Looking down, Angie's attention is diverted from the scampering dog as she glances over at her mother's feet. "Wait a sec. What is that?" Angie asks, letting out a light scream. She points at her mother's ankle.

Sue turns her foot away, so Angie can't see the small tattoo of an artist's brush inside her right ankle.

"I go off to school and come back to find I have Deborah Harry for a mom?"

"Your dad thinks it's kind of naughty," Sue says in a sheepish tone.

"Mom, have you ever heard of TMI—too much info?"

Sue goes to the refrigerator and starts taking out deli meats, bread, cheese, lettuce, and condiments.

"I'll make some of my special construction-worker sandwiches," calls Cliff from the living room. "I'm just checking the scores on ESPN. Gotta see if BC is going to a bowl game."

Sue looks at Angie and they share a conspiratorial look. Sue reaches into the bottom shelf and takes out a mixed berry pie. Miming a cutting action with a knife while pointing to the silverware drawer, she takes two plates down from a cabinet and gestures toward the kitchen table with her head. "We might as well get a lead on dessert, then," she half whispers.

Angie and Sue descend upon the kitchen table, each grabbing a chair. Sue spins around the chair at the head of the table and Angie throws her legs up on it. Sue pats Angie's feet.

"I'm so glad you're home, sweetie. Now tell me, how's Sarah? She still crazy as ever?" asks Sue.

Angie smiles and makes a sigh of exhaustion. "You don't know the half of it."

"Well, how's that boy—Jack, right? Um, you kids going out or anything?"

"Kinda, sorta, I guess." Angie digs into her pie and focuses on just the right amount of berries, crust, and vanilla ice cream for the perfect bite. Sue silently watches her and smiles.

"Hey, Mom, I have to ask you something. I know it's going to sound crazy and believe me, I've been thinking about this for a long time." Angie hesitates and moves her dessert about, scraping the fork back and forth. Sue slides her chair closer to the table and leans forward, resting on her elbows. Angie raises her eyebrows as she watches her mother's movements. "Ah, you know what? Never mind," says Angie. Sue stops sipping her tea, putting the cup down quickly.

"Come on, Angie. What? Tell me. Come on, you and I talk about everything. Is it about Jack?" She raises her ankle, showing her tattoo again. "I'm considered hip these days."

She points to it. "See that? Exhibit A. So, you can tell me anything and I will get it and not judge. C'mon, I watch the Kardashians. I know what's up."

Angie attempts to throw a serious look at Sue, but they break out in simultaneous laughter, causing Angie to spew some of her pie onto the table in a goopy wad. She gets up, goes over to the sink, and grabs some paper towels to scoop it up.

"Sorry, Mom," she says in a half-strangled whisper, pie remnants lodged in her windpipe.

"Not a problem," says Sue. "You OK?" Their relationship, so strained and contentious during Angie's adolescence, has settled into a comfortable friendship.

Angie is coughing, and Daisy, her sense of smell fully activated by the recognition of the possible opportunity for scavenging, comes back into the kitchen and scurries around the tangle of chairs, table, and human legs. Angie steps back from the sink and accidentally steps on her paw. Daisy lets out a wounded screech that startles both Angie and Sue. "Oh, my wittle Daisy, come here, girlie," says Sue, as if cooing to a baby. Daisy's tail is between her legs as she cautiously makes her way into Sue's arms. Daisy is bombarded with kisses on the paws from Sue and Angie.

"Do I need to call PETA on you two?" asks Cliff at the kitchen door.

"No, Dad, we've decided not to make a pair of gloves out of Daisy, so there's no cause for concern," Angie shoots back.

"Okay, good. I guess we can get on with dinner, huh? Hey, what are you guys doing? Is this the college way or something, eating dessert first? Or are you just worried your old man will get to the pie first?"

"I think you just answered your own question, dear," says Sue.

"Well, hope you have some room left for the main course, 'cause here comes the hero of the hero sandwiches. Now you're gonna see how Daddy rolls with the rolls!"

"Wow, Dad. You try this hard at school? Because you're more corny beef at this point than anything else."

"Never mind, Clarke girls. Just step out of the way and let a master perform his magic. Observe, ladies, as Reuben Hoagie, aka Sloppy Joe, the Hero Grinder, jumps on his gyro-guided torpedoed submarine and transforms the mundane into the gastrolicious, the magnificent, the mouthwatering, the belch-inducing, and jaw-stretching...sandwich of Earl!" With a dramatic flourish, Cliff swiftly opens four jars of condiments while simultaneously undoing a bag of sandwich rolls. He unwraps several baggies of ham, roast beef, and American cheese, and begins to slice the rolls and lather mayonnaise, Gulden's mustard, some relish, and some roasted red peppers on either side of the open rolls. "And, now, the main act." He rolls up three thick slabs of meat wrapped around several slices of cheese, and inserts these clumps into each bun. He pivots and moves toward the table, tries to grasp all three plates waiter-style and make his way to the table without incident, but luck is not on his side. Angie and Sue laugh at his amateur circus act, as a jar of pickles he's clamped between his forearms slips and escapes his grasp. Cliff tries to catch the falling jar with his knees, which he somehow does, but in doing so loses control of everything else. He manages to force the three plates over the table with a lurching heave, whereupon they fall with a clatter. Nothing's broken except for his pride.

"What?" he says. "I was trying to do that."

"Angie, you think it's easy living with him? There's a place in heaven for me," Sue says, mostly to herself.

As Cliff retrieves and redistributes all of the sandwich materials, Angie goes to the liquor cabinet, takes out a bottle of red wine, gets two glasses, and brings them over to the table. Cliff and Sue exchange glances with each other as Angie remains stoic. Angie opens the bottle and pours two glasses of wine, one for herself and a surprised Sue.

"When did you start drinking wine?" asks Sue.

"High school," mutters Angie. "C'mon, Mom. If we're going to talk, let's lube the works a wee bit. You know, when Dad plays golf, he'll have a couple of beers, calls it swing oil.

Well, this is ours." She sits, pours, and they join her at the table, each with a sandwich and a glass of wine, and Cliff with a beer. Daisy, sensing opportunity lost, waddles to a spot in the corner of the kitchen, curls up, sighs, and closes one eye, the other one still hopeful that gravity will give her bounty.

After a few bites, Sue opens the topic all know has to be opened.

"So. You're home."

"Yeeeah, Mom, I am home. What, you plan on renting my room out or something? Or better yet, plan on turning it into a media center or man cave for Dad?"

"No, dear, let's get on topic here. You're not ducking out of this."

"Okay. You want to know why I'm home and what's going on? You sure you're ready?" Angie grabs a strand of hair and brings it under her nose, where she twirls it and bounces the ends lightly against the soft tissue between her nostrils.

When Sue sees this routine, she smiles and slowly blinks her eyes, but doesn't say anything. She and Cliff exchange a telling glance.

"Remember that older guy, Mr. Fife, from town who died at the golf course?" Angie continues. Sue nods as she takes a sip of wine. "Okay, now for the bomb. I don't think he died under normal circumstances. I don't pretend to know what happened, but I don't think—no, I know—it wasn't normal. I know it sounds really crazy, and imagine me getting involved in something like this. I mean, I know I'm not taking criminology or anything, but—"

"Criminology?" Sue interrupts with a half shout. "What are you talking about, criminology? Criminology involves, well, you know, crime. If there's a crime, you have no business getting involved in anything other than watching *CSI*. You are a student, Angie. *That's* what you are, at least for the next six months."

"Whoa, Mom, chill. You haven't heard it all. I have a good idea why this whole thing is happening. I was at school and the exact same thing happened there that happened to Mr. Fife. So, I went to this lady's funeral and the service was just so…I don't know…inspiring. Weird, but inspiring. There was this little girl who is related to her and she was in a wheelchair, and this black guy who was wheeling her who…I don't know how to put it, but he had this…presence about him, almost like an aura, you know? And he and the little girl both winked at me, and I know it meant something."

"Hey! You didn't tell me anything about any man winking at you, Angie," Cliff interjects.

"Dad, it wasn't that kind of a wink. It was a wink like he *knew* something, as if he had some special wisdom or something, and he wanted me to know what that something was, too."

"Angela Grace Clarke, you told me this was a story and that you were going to see what you could find out about it and then get your behind back to school," Cliff says, halfway between annoyance and exasperation.

"Dad, Mom, you know, you guys always told me that you can't live your life in a bottle, that you should be aware of what's going on around you and get involved. You taught me to be a good citizen and be kind. Well, I'm doing just that. I'm just not sure how to go about doing it." Angie looks for a reaction from her parents, but there is nothing. "It's so obvious to me and I'm so confused why no one else can see it." Seeing no reaction—and judging from their blank faces, there is none forthcoming—she continues in a quieter tone. "All right, I'm definitely freaked by the whole thing, but I have to be honest with you guys, this is what it is to be a reporter. I do get a rush from knowing something other people don't, and from trying to figure out how to prove it and then tell it. This feels like the real thing."

"Honey, you need to…" Sue starts to say something but Cliff interrupts.

"Sue, hold on. Angie, listen up. You have a couple of days, like I told you before. And if you are going to pursue this, and I have the feeling you would do so even if we placed you under house arrest and chained you to your bureau, then you have to promise me you will go and talk to Mr. Armstrong and get his advice on how to go forward. And it wouldn't hurt to have the paper behind you, you know."

"Uh, yeah, sure," says Angie, quickly sensing this is her best opportunity to win parental blessing for her chosen mission. "I will."

"Promise?"

"Promise, Dad."

"Cliff, I'm just not sure about this," says Sue.

Winking at Angie from the side of his face only she can see, he says, "I'm sure between us and Mr. Armstrong, with all his sources and contacts, we can keep our budding Diane Sawyer safe and on the path."

Angie, grateful for her father's validation, practically leaps across the table to hug him. "Dad, thanks," she says into his neck. Pulling back, she looks over at her mother. "Mom, believe me, no one values my safety more than I do. And I can show everyone how good a reporter I can be, while still coming home to stop you from overfeeding my dog."

"Your dog?" says her mother. "Who's been watching him for the past three and a half years?"

Feeling the mood shift to a more comfortable, mundane one, Angie rolls her eyes and responds, "You have, Mom. I know, I know. Hey, who's up for a little movie time? Let's see what's on TV? Dad, want to join us for a couple chick flicks on Netflix?"

"Thanks, honey, for the offer," he says. "You two go ahead and get a little vicarious romance. I'll just clean up and read about the Civil War. Can't know too much about how old Stonewall deployed the troops. I have a classroom of hungry warmongers to keep interested on Monday."

CHAPTER 9

Press or Pull

Monday morning at a weekly newspaper is really more like midweek for its reporters, editors, ad reps, and other staffers. Coming out on a Thursday, a weekly's work cycle begins, for the most part, on a Friday. The Wednesday noon deadline looms like an overlarge speed bump midway through everyone else's "normal" workweek. While most of the workforce is starting off with sprightly waltz, a weekly news staff is already doing the jitterbug. This can result in short fuses among coworkers, and long days while the news staff writes up stories about land use, town governance, school board meetings, amusing cat rescues, horrendous or traffic-choking car accidents, and the fully involved structure fires. A human interest feature on someone performing an invaluable service to the community, an appropriately warm and fuzzy piece on the ladies auxiliary quilt-making subcommittee, or the Lions Club used-eyeglasses drive helps round out the material that wraps around the advertisements that pay for the ink and paper it's all printed on. Everything that will appear in Thursday's *Advocate* is in the process of being gathered in notes, camera cards, and manifest sheets, in preparation for each of the stories, photos, and advertising displays. All of it is tossed into the top part of a funnel, and the tip of the funnel is the production department, which begins to scream for product to push through just after the caffeine takes effect at eight thirty in the morning.

And so it is into this maelstrom of activity. Angie arrives shortly after nine o'clock, after a pleasantly spent Sunday with her mom and dad. She enters the building just in time to hear the first salvo thrown at Pip Peters, the staff photographer, by advertising director Alice Watt, who, in her best impersonation of a fearsome substitute teacher, is demanding shrilly to know "when the hell those Santa Claus shots from that smelly Boys and Girls Club are going to be in my e-mail. You said they'd be ready this morning."

"It *is* morning, Alice," Pip answers. "We've got another three hours to go in order for me to stay within the promised time frame," he adds, grinning at her back as she strides away to her own office.

After witnessing the door to Alice's office being slammed shut, Angie looks at Brenda and Pip, who share a knowing glance with each other before turning their attention toward her. "Some things never change, I guess," Angie offers.

"No, some things never do," says Brenda. "Alice tries to control everyone."

"And everything *about* everyone," adds Pip.

"And our artistically tempered Peter here revolts the only way he knows how—by being a little…"

Pip jumps back in. "By making her realize how wrong she is and how right I am."

"By being passive-aggressive and hiding behind the fact that Bill happens to like him," continues Brenda.

"He loves me because there is no better shooter in the commonwealth, and I have the awards to prove it," finishes Pip.

"Like I said, some things never change," says Angie. "Humor, humility, and all the news that fits in print."

"Right, Ange. All the news that gives us fits," says Brenda. "Now what are you doing here on a Monday morning? School isn't out yet, is it? I feel like we just saw you."

"No, fall semester is marching right along to its parade-grounds review—what we call finals because they are, well, final," Angie says. "But anyway, I'm taking a couple of days off so I can do a follow-up on that Charlie Fife story."

"That's still a story?" Pip asks. "Thought they figured he wandered off on a late night jingle-bell joyride. You know, when old elephants get sick and they know they're going to die, they just head for the hills alone to go check out. Maybe he was just an old elephant."

"Pip, sometimes you should zip your lip and leave the words buried in the dark hole from which they spring," says a gravelly voice behind the three at the reception area. Bill Armstrong, arms crossed over a black, green, and red Argyle sweater, is standing there, reading glasses perched professorially at the tip of his nose, shooting a shameful gaze at his photographer, chin jutting forward. "You finished up for the week so soon, or are you trolling for a severance package? I don't believe water-cooler gossip is in your best interest. What do you think?"

"No, Bill, I mean Mr. Armstrong, I was just telling the ladies how psyched I am to go shoot the teens at the Arlington Fidelity House this afternoon, after I crop Alice's Christmas gift guide this morning," Pip says. "In fact, I was just heading to my computer."

Bill watches him leave, shaking his head in a small gesture before turning his attention to Angie. "What in God's name are you doing here, Ms. Clarke? Get kicked out of school?"

"No, Mr. Armstrong, I mean, Bill," Angie says, trying to sound confident but failing. "Actually, I'm here to talk to you. I know it's coming up on deadline, so I won't take long, if you have just a few minutes, I—"

"Yeah, yeah, I know, just a few minutes for a discussion big enough to keep you out of school before exams," Bill interrupts. "C'mon, talk while I edit our guest columnists and letter writers." He turns on his heels and strides toward his office, Angie in tow.

Letting himself into his chair with a rear-pointing free fall, Bill grunts as a compressed hiss of air escapes the seat cushion on his fake leather upholstered chair. He pats an arm of the offending chair. "Gotta love Naugahyde. It excuses an infinite number of abuses. Spills, stains, and trapped gases— all dissipate or get wiped away. You ever wonder about the 'Nauga'? What its natural history is? Where it lives? What it eats? Whether it gives birth to live young or produces eggs like a duck-billed platypus?"

"Uh, I'm not sure I ever heard of it," says Angie.

"No? Well, it's plastic," Bill says, turning toward his computer screen and clicking his mouse several times impatiently. "It was developed as a pleather, a plastic composite with a knit fabric backing, and a PVC coating that was made to imitate leather while costing less and requiring less care. The term 'Nauga' was an overly cute marketing campaign that used cheap Muppet-like stuffed animals to help sell the material as a furniture covering. Now pleather resides in dentists' offices, airports, and diners everywhere." He points to a chair next to his desk. "There, sit in that. It's made out of something called 'wood.'"

Eyebrows raised and mouth open, Angie sits and says, "How do you know stuff like that? Is it part of the job?"

"Exactly, young lady," Bill says, peering at his computer monitor. "Did a story on the move of the company that made it, US Rubber, from its original home in Naugatuck, Connecticut, to Wisconsin. Worked at the *Waterbury Republican-American* at the time. It was my first posting as an editor. Before I entered into glorious semiretirement as the helmsman of this here Goof Ship Lollipop. Now, young lady, what are you doing here?"

"Well, I'm not sure where to begin with this," Angie says tentatively, as if exploring a darkened room.

"If you can't begin a story, Angie, you might as well be in the wrong business. Just start talking. Words tend to happen that way. Spit a few out, they turn into phrases, and—"

"Right, Bill," interrupts Angie, smiling faintly. "I remember. 'Words turn into phrases, which turn into sentences, which turn into paragraphs, which turn into the beginnings, middles, and ends of a story.' Really, you should be a professor at my school."

Bill nods, turns in his chair to face Angie, and cocks his head at an angle while extending his arms and turning his hands over, palms up, as if in an offering. "Soooo…start talking."

"Remember the Charlie Fife story? How he died over at the golf course, out in the snow next to a sled? At Thanksgiving? Remember how weird that was, that a man his age would even be out that late at night, much less in the snow with a sled?" Angie's words, once started, come tumbling out, like marbles from a bag.

"Yes, Angie, I remember. Old Charlie. There are—were—three Charlies; Junior and Chas are the son and grandson. Short-term memory's slowing down, but it's not stopped yet. Go on."

"Okay. Well, up at Syracuse last week, the same thing happened. Only this time, it was an old woman who died. Same way—in the snow, sledding, late at night. Same kind of sled, even—a Flexible Flyer. Police gave the same 'explanation' of exposure to the elements," Angie continues, making air quotes with her index fingers extended in front of her face.

"All right, that's a repetition of a puzzling event," says Armstrong. "But a strange event plus another strange event add up to two unusual events, which could, and in fact most likely does, equal nothing more than a coincidence. What else? The look on your face tells me there's more."

"Well, I had a hunch, so I went to the funeral service and then the burial. And it was amazing. She—her name was Helen Thompson—was a devoted mother and grandmother, active in the community, and everybody knew her and liked her. Just like Charlie Fife. And she had a granddaughter, who was at the...okay, I see you looking at me funny, but she was special, Bill, really. There was something about her and the way she picked me out. And then—get this—the granddaughter and her caregiver, the guy who wheeled her into and out of the church and put her in her van, they *winked* at me." She stops, letting the statement sink in.

"Some guy winks at you and you're onto a story? Girl, that's the oldest story in the world. Necessary story, yes, to keep the human race going, but sometimes it's just a story of hormones run amok. Was the guy young, old, cute, homely, creepy, or what?"

"Bill, it wasn't like that. First off, it was hard to tell how old he was. He looked youngish, thirties to middle-aged, somewhere in there. But that's not the point. It wasn't a sexual kind of wink, it was more like a 'I know who you are' kind of wink. And they *both* winked at me, and made this gesture with their thumb and forefinger," Angie says, clicking them together. "It made me feel like they knew who I was, why I was there, and that they were leading me onward."

"Did they talk to you, give you a card to call them or anything?"

"No. They took off right after the funeral, but I know they were trying to tell me I was on the right track by being there."

"And what exactly, or even close to exactly, do you think that track is? Murder and mayhem? Are they both perps acting in tandem, or are they reluctant witnesses trying to warn you of a wicked plot? Is the girl in the wheelchair acting in cahoots with the middle-aged winker, or is she held unwillingly in his sociopathic sway while he coverers up a murder in the snow and maybe even plotting yet another sledding death? Does she even need to be in a wheelchair, or is that just a really convenient cover? And all this while winking at cub reporters in a graveyard?"

"I don't know, Bill, but I'm serious. If you think you can throw me off by making fun of my story idea and me, I'll do it on my own. But I *did* research what I could and I did find there was a probable connection to why the girl is in a wheelchair. The family asked that donations be given in the name of Mrs. Thompson to the SMA foundation. It's a disease, a group of diseases, actually, called spinal muscular atrophy that attacks motor neurons of the spinal cord and brain stem. It's a genetic mutation that results in weakness in the muscles that aid in swallowing, breathing, and in the victim's limbs. Anywhere from one in six thousand to one in…"

"Twenty thousand people are affected," Bill finishes. "It ranges from relatively benign to severe."

Angie pauses, looks wonderingly at her mentor. "I can't believe you know that, too," she says, shaking her head.

"Only reason I know is because I looked into it recently, too. You establish a direct link between this girl and SMA? You sure the girl has it, or is she in the chair for some other reason?"

"No, I didn't make that call yet. I wanted to wait and see what else I could dig up before I tipped my hand."

"Good girl. Know when to hold them, know when to fold them, and know when to show them."

"Right, Bill. I know, I know. And know if you bluff that you'll have to get them talking. Believe me, I am so into this. And I know I got something."

"Okay, let's assume you are onto something. My question for you is, did you ever look into what I told you about Old Charlie's grandson?"

Angie stares at Bill blankly for about five seconds. Then she sits up straight in her chair and claps her hands on her knees. "That's right, he was in braces!" she exclaims. She raises one hand, index finger pointed in the air, turns it to point at her temple, cocks her thumb, and mimes shooting herself in the head. "What a dope! I never did check. I just wrote the story about Old Charlie's death and what people said about him in a sidebar feature. I never talked to his grandson. I felt funny calling him while he was grieving."

"Well, you are *not* a dope, Angie, but you *are* still a rookie. A talented rookie, but a rookie nonetheless. Making those tough calls are what makes a good story a great story, and a good reporter a great reporter. Getting past the so-called 'shame' of intruding on someone at a sensitive moment is when you'll know you can write about anything and anyone at anytime. Most of the time, people want to talk, to share their thoughts and let their feelings and motivations be known. They aren't seeing you as you, Angie Clarke. They are seeing their peers, relatives, friends, and foes, and you aren't that important to them. You are only a conduit to their truths. Or maybe to their lies. But after you do that once, you'll be free to be the great reporter that's inside you."

"Gee, thanks for making me feel better, Bill," Angie says quietly, blushing slightly. "Hey," she says, her voice sharpening. "You said you looked up SMA recently. Why?"

Grinning widely, Bill raises a hand, palm outstretched over his head, and thrusts it toward Angie. "High five! I knew you'd get there, Lois Lane. I looooove seeing that light go on in a cubby's eyes." They slap palms. "Well, we have ourselves another coincidence here, which makes three coincidences, which is two more than is statistically probable. One, old people in the snow. Two, Flexible Flyers near their bodies.

And now, number three. Chas, Old Charlie's grandson, has SMA too. Didn't think much of it until you mentioned the Thompson kid up in the 'Frozen 'Cuse,' well, not much of it other than it's too bad the kid—any kid—has it. Now, this still doesn't mean anything is afoot concerning these two deaths, but it does make it more interesting."

Angie begins to twirl her hair. "So we call the Fight SMA people, and see if we can get a list of donations made that coincide with deaths around the country, and see if we can match them?"

"Well, maybe. Tough to get records from nonprofits. Need a wagon full of lawyers pulled by a team of politicians feeding exclusively on money. We can make the calls straight up to see if they respond. Meanwhile, do a Nexis search—"

"Yeah, I started one up at school, but stuff came up and I—"

"I know, I know. By 'stuff' you mean you actually acted like a college kid. I put two kids through college, Ange, I know 'stuff' comes up. But there is one more thing that's been cooking on the back burner up here," he says, tapping his temple. "Thought it was just happenstance that led nowhere, and it still might not be anything, but…"

"What, Bill, what?" Angie asks, insistent.

"Keep in mind what I tell you was given to me off the record. We can't use it unless we get corroboration, and that's not likely, at least not here. We have a deal? No passing this on? To anyone. And by anyone, I mean you don't even mouth the words to yourself while you look in the mirror tonight. Or tomorrow morning, or anytime."

"Yes, Bill. I know the Code. Go ahead."

"All right. Someone in the police department told me there was something weird at the scene where Old Charlie died." He pauses, waits one beat too long, a smirk starting to play across his face.

Angie's impatience surfaces briefly as Bill draws out his silence. "Weird how?" she blurts, cutting her question short, trying to sound cool.

"As in inexplicable, as in baffling, as in peculiar." He stops talking, drumming his fingers on the arms of his chair, clearly enjoying the moment.

"Okay, Bill, okay! C'mon! What do you want from me? Tell me what you heard. Heck, I'll wash your car every day all next summer. Just tell me!"

"Hopefully, you'll be too busy writing to wash anything but your hair once a week, but thanks, anyway. Okay, here goes. And keep in mind this is like Twilight Zone stuff, or to stay more within your age group, Harry Potter stuff. So the police pretty much dismissed it. As they probably should have." He pauses again.

"Bill, I will kill you. Stop toying and spill facts, will you?"

He regards her for a second. "They found footprints on the approach to the hill on the fifteenth fairway that matched Old Charlie's boots. That they expected. They also found his footprints going up the actual hill. There were the footmarks you would expect at the top where he would have set down and positioned the sled. The snow was tramped down there at the crest, just as you would expect with a sledder trying to clear a platform for taking off. Then there was a clear trail left by the sled, two sharp lines divided by smoothed-down snow, sitting lower than the snow outside the lines left by the sled's runners. All this you would expect from someone out for a solo sled ride."

Bill lets the statement sit there as Angie raises her left eyebrow. "And?"

"There was another pair of footprints. They came up from the other side of the hill and their impressions did not match Old Charlie's footprints. In fact, the difference was pretty dramatic. Charlie's boot prints had treads, the others did not. They were smooth. No distinct heel markings, either. Just smooth, flat footprints."

"Did they take an imprint?"

"No, they measured the prints, though. Size ten, indicating a male. Lets Bigfoot off the hook. And all but really large women."

"Why would someone go out in the snow and ice with flat shoes? Not very practical or outdoorsy," Angie says.

"I don't know. Smooth soles, clean soul? That's not the weirdest thing about the prints, though. Old Charlie's footprints led away from the crest of the hill toward where the second pair of footprints ends. The two pair point toward each other from two feet, eight and a quarter inches. Then, a pair of Old Charlie's footprints led back toward the sledding platform. Alone."

Angie sits still, digesting the information. "What about the other footprints? Where did they go next?"

Bill nods. "Aha, there's the rub—nowhere. They just stop there, two feet, eight and a quarter inches away from Old Charlie's, and go nowhere. Poof. As if whoever left them walked backward from where they came or was airlifted from the spot by helicopter. Or giant eagle. Or maybe a pterodactyl."

Angie seizes a turn to take a swipe at Bill. "Quetzalcoatlus, Bill. Pterodactyls were actually too small. Quetzalcoatluses were the pterosaurs big enough to hoist a human being into the air. So what do the cops think this all means?"

"They don't know what it means. The impressions left in the snow by Old Charlie's boots are just as deep going up to meet the other footprints as they are going back to the sled, so there's no reason to think he carried that person on his back. And there was no sign of any kind of struggle. Just isolated footprints leading up to each other in the bare snow. No blood, no hair, no broken-off fingernails, no sticks, no samurai swords—nothing. Just virgin snow between the footprints. And so no proof there was ever any real meeting between Charlie and…whomever those one-way footprints belonged to. Theoretically the footprints could have been made by each walker at different times."

Angie takes a pad and pen from her handbag, crosses her legs, uncaps the pen, and flips the pad open to a blank page. "How far away were the meeting footprints from the spot where they found Charlie Fife's body?" she asks.

"Good question. A hundred and eighty-four feet."

"Could the treadless footprints have been covered over at the spot of death by Charlie's footprints?"

"Ah, probably not."

"Probably?"

"Well, they found a lot of other footprints down at the bottom. Some left by the guy out walking the golf course who found the body, some belonged to EMT guys, and probably some belonged to the first cop on the scene, but they wouldn't ever admit to that, being pros and all. Oh, and a bunch of dog footprints. Local groundskeeper has a black Lab, and says the dog was out that night. Didn't think much of it, though."

"They do any blood work on Old Charlie, a toxicology test?"

"No, the family didn't want one. They just wanted to bury Charlie. And the cops didn't make enough out of the mystery prints to deem them worthy of forcing the issue. Popular family, well-respected older man, no known enemies, no sign of foul play. Not enough added up to suspect anything other than a foolish late-night adventure by someone too old for foolishness. I would agree with them, even given your weird other sledding death. But a similar SMA connection and the footprints to nowhere make my ears perk up. Didn't happen to hear if they found any mystery prints up in the 'Cuse?"

"There wasn't anything in the paper or on TV," Angie answers.

"If there were, the cops might have held that out of the press for the same reason Arlington's did. Withholding information to winnow a potential suspect from a crackpot. If I were you, I'd check with the Syracuse cops. At least get them on the record."

Angie smiles. "So you think there's a story here, too, don't you?"

"Don't know. Can't know unless you look. But remember, a theory advanced is a thesis. Its contradiction is the antithesis. A combination is called a synthesis and it is the road to truth. Now what's your plan of approach?"

"I guess talk to the family. Families. The SMA people. Look for more 'coincidences.' Sniff around the Syracuse

Police Department, see if they found any footprints. Can you think of anything else?"

"No, I'd say start with those. Now, you will have a good reason other than your grades to go back to Syracuse, won't you? Give it a day or two here checking out the other leads, and then back you go."

"All right, Bill, I will. So can I use the name of the paper when I introduce myself to people I'm calling, even though I'm not a regular staff reporter?"

"Yes, Angie, you can say you work for the *Advocate*. And I'll do what I can to help, but I can't spare the staff to send anyone in the field. Need them to cover the zoning variances for the neighborhood watchers and scintillating things like that. But remember to tread carefully when you ask questions. Don't give away too much, don't sound like you are doing anything but a routine follow-up on charities and the like. Ease into the questions and save the hard hitters for the end of the interview. Let the silence sit there if anyone takes too long to answer a question. Fools rush in to fill the silence when it becomes uncomfortable, and they may give more away if you make them think they need to be that fool filling the silence. And above all, don't forget to ask the second why."

"The second why? What's that mean?"

"Ah, a lesson I didn't force onto your clean plate during your internship? The second why is when you have gotten an answer, and you don't feel it's deep enough or complete enough, that they may have more to say if you keep prompting them. You do it by pretending you're dumb, as in, 'Gee, I'm not sure how these dirty dishes move from the sink to the dishwasher every time?' Or you can ask it another way, from another angle, like, 'Sometimes I see your mother load the dishwasher and she sees me. Why is it we only see you and your sister put dirty dishes in the sink and never in the dishwasher?' And if you still don't think it's a complete answer, ask why a third time."

"Ahhh," says Angie. "The second why. Always plan a second why. Got it."

"Well, Angie, deadline approaches. And you know why they call it deadline, don't you?"

"Because in the old days, the telegraph line went dead at a given time, and the paper couldn't get printed if the line wasn't up and going?"

"No, Angie. No one knows, because everyone who ever missed one in this business was executed and dead men don't talk. Now, go dig up what you can and stay in touch." He turns back to his computer screen as Angie gets up to leave. "And stay safe, or I will personally kill you."

Angie heads toward the door. As she reaches it, Bill stops her. "Hey, Angie."

"What, Bill?"

"Quetzalcoatlus. How'd you know that? You do a paper on dinosaurs?"

"No, it was on *Dino Dan*. Nickelodeon. We watch TV sometimes in the lounge before dinner." She leaves Bill shaking his head and laughing softly to himself.

CHAPTER 10

Dreamsicle

B ack in her car, Angie starts her engine, allowing it to go through its startup routine, rumbling through its progression of phlegmatic mechanical phrasings as it reluctantly coughs itself into wakefulness. After cranking the blower to max, she sits back, begins twirling her hair, and thinks about her next step. *Call Syracuse Police Department first, and see if there were any smooth-soled solitary footprints near Helen Thompson. Call the Fifes and see if they knew Old Charlie was going sledding and if they solicited donations for SMA after*

he died. Do a search again for more elderly deaths under similar circumstances. Hmm. What else?

She Googles the main number for nonemergency calls for the Syracuse Police Department on her iPhone, finds it, and turns off the car radio, which she realizes, with some irony, might as well have not been playing anything at all, and makes the phone call. *I need to stay on task*, she tells herself as she rehearses what she is going to say and how she is going to say it.

"Syracuse Police. How can I help you?" asks a voice that manages to sound both feminine and mechanical at the same time.

"Hi, my name is Angie Clarke, and I'm a reporter for the *Arlington Advocate* in Arlington, Massachusetts, and we are looking into a death of an elderly man here in town that has some similarities to a death of an elderly woman that occurred up in Syracuse, and I'd like to talk to someone about it."

"You'll have to talk to Deputy Chief Welch about any ongoing murder investigations," says the woman.

"Well, I don't know if it is something that's being investigated," says Angie, feeling driven off-track from her planned line of inquiry almost as soon as it began.

"Any open or currently not active investigation still goes through the Investigations Bureau, and you'll have to talk to the deputy chief about it," says the woman, already looking to shed a pesky reporter.

"Is he in?"

"No, *she* is not in. I'll put you to her voice mail," says the dispatcher, having successfully taken the call to its end.

Following the abrupt prompt on the deputy chief's machine, Angie, feeling rushed, blurts her message: "Hi, my name is Angie Clarke, and I am a reporter looking into a couple of cases where old—uh, elderly—people died while sledding, and there was one up in Syracuse a couple of weeks ago, and I have some questions about the case, and would like to talk to someone up there about it. My number is seven-eight-one, six-four-three, two-four-eight-three. Thanks."

Feeling slightly foolish and frustrated at not seizing control of the call as she had been coached by Bill and taught in class, Angie punches END CALL, puts her phone in her parka pocket, and sighs, sitting back in the car seat and leaning her head against the headrest. She looks around at the people walking by the parking lot, gathers herself, and with another sigh, she sits back up straight and backs out of the lot. Navigating her way through town, she heads north on Mystic Street, looking out onto the partly frozen Mystic Lake, where a gathering of ducks and geese bobs, dives, and jockeys for position in the open section of the water's expanse. As she reaches the Winchester Golf Course, she pulls into the clubhouse lot and looks out on the deserted course. *It sure looks different white than green*, she thinks. Following a heavily trodden group of footprints partly filled in by a more recent snowfall, she makes her way around a thicket of trees and scrubs toward the sloping fifteenth fairway. Looking up where Old Charlie would have sledded, she imagines what he likely saw and felt as he approached.

He would have felt a little heavy and lethargic from his Thanksgiving meal. And he had gone to a noon game earlier in the day with his grandson, Chas. He probably got treated a little like a conquering hero at the game, which would offset any embarrassment he might have felt for Chas having to walk through the crowd with leg braces. Or maybe he used a wheelchair? She takes off her gloves and takes out a pad, rubbing her pen across the cardboard backing to get the ink going, and makes a note to check on the wheelchair. "No detail too obscure," she says out loud, summoning her self-confidence. The wind moves through a stand of trees, making a small roar. A branch creaks. It sounds like a bone breaking.

Putting her gloves back on and her notebook in her back pocket, Angie trudges up the hill, taking care to look around as she makes her way up along the margins of where countless numbers of saucers, sleds, and pieces of cardboard have journeyed since the night Old Charlie died. Her L.L Bean boots slide a little on the worn part of the slope, which causes her to think about the physics of the trip. *Whoa, that's too weird, even for fiction. Even Professor K couldn't explain this. Ange, get a grip.*

Continuing up toward the brow of the hill, Angie's not really sure where the rough, or the fairway, ends and the green begins. She can only tell where the sand traps are because their contours make large scoops out of the landscape, as if cleaved out by a giant ice cream dipper. As she reaches the rim of the crest, Angie feels the colder air of the snow being lifted by the wind, making her eyes water and her cheeks sting. She looks down the hill, trying to imagine the scene at night. *No one around, except for a clean soled man or woman*, she thinks, amused at her pun. *Was there any light at all? I'd better try to check out what the night sky was like after midnight.*

Angie takes a few aimless steps around the area, trying to figure out which of the prints might be leftovers from the night Old Charlie died. *There are so many footprints now, and some of them are filled in by new snow. This is telling me nothing. What am I missing?*

Her phone, buried in an inside parka pocket, begins to throb and warble. The song "Moves Like Jagger" becomes recognizable, indicating a call or text. Fingers thickened by gloves and numbed by cold, Angie fumbles with the outside zipper and then the inside pocket. By the time she extracts it, the message has been left, and she removes her gloves again, and hits the app to read it. "GKTW" is the message.

Who the heck? That's the second time and there's no return number. Weird.

Angie looks around to see if anyone's watching. She alternates glances at the screen with a visual scouring of the horizon. Finally, she pockets the phone, zips up, and looks off in both directions, studying the trees for anomalies or movement. Everything looks like an anomaly, or as if it's something moving that shouldn't be moving. Finally satisfied that what she is imagining to be sinister isn't, Angie heads on down the hill. *Technology isn't perfect, I guess*, she thinks. The wind has stopped. She continues wandering around the hillcrest.

"Just shoot for the stars, if it feels right, and aim for my heart, if you feel like." Maroon 5 again. Technology isn't perfect or imperfect; it just is.

Angie tries to make herself invisible. She is frozen still, not from the cold—from fear. Part of her wants to know what is on her phone this time, part of her doesn't. Curiosity wins out. She pulls out her phone and looks at it. "GKTW," reads the text.

Now I am officially spooked. This is messed up and I am creeped out. She continues her walk down the hill. Fear seeps through her, spreading from her center to her extremities like water through sand. It seems to her as if she is moving in slow motion, as if she has been suddenly transported to a planet in which gravity is three times stronger than Earth's.

She speeds up, begins to sweat, her heartbeats pounding in her ears. Forty feet to the car. Thirty feet to the car. Twenty. Ten. Finally there. Now inside.

Once she's in her car, Angie feels a little less exposed, a little safer, but she can still feel her hands shaking as she points the key toward the ignition and misses—twice. She gets the key in the lock on the third try and starts it up, pleased that it seems uncommonly cooperative. Putting the car into gear and spinning out of the icy parking lot, Angie feels her fear hissing out of her gut, like air escaping from a balloon. She makes a show of looking both ways before heading out onto the road that will take her home. Warmed by the car heater, which has shifted into overdrive and been wearied by her trek, she begins to feel a little more at ease. *I'll feel even better when I'm home. Or maybe I should go to the police. And tell them what? I'm getting texted? Oh, boy, that'd get them calling in the FBI for help, I bet. No, maybe I should just keep this to myself.*

Turning on the radio, Angie makes a conscious choice to go new pop and flips on 108 KISS-FM, hoping for something sugary to get her mind off her recent encounter on the hill. She's relieved, nonetheless, to get "Someone Like You" by Adele. "Well, she sure has chops," mimicking Randy Jackson from *American Idol*. By the time she pulls in front of her house, her heartbeat is back to normal and her hands are no longer shaking. She is both relieved and disappointed there's no one home—not that she would expect anyone to be at one in the afternoon on a workday—wishing there was someone around to help her feel safe but glad she doesn't have to talk about what happened. She goes in the house and locks the door behind her. *Just in case,* she assures herself. She fixes herself a bowl of Cheerios, which she spoons down while standing at the kitchen counter by the sink, and drinks a glass of orange juice to wash it down.

Temporarily satiated, Angie takes a glass of milk with her up to her room, gets her ThinkPad out, and plops down on her bed, propping the computer on a pillow so she's better able to type. Typing up her notes from the day, and revisiting the suggested lines of inquiry she got from her meeting with Bill, Angie feels a sense of accomplishment, more in control and comfortably in her element. She puts her head back and begins to feel the emotional and physical toll herding her toward sleep. Bringing herself back to wakefulness when she catches herself making a few tentative snoring honks, she tries to stay awake, but soon succumbs to sleep and into a weird, dreamy state.

The light from the bright moon illuminates Charlie Fife's house. Its rays stream through the scattered snowflakes, and a bluish light filters into his bedroom, casting some form and dimension to objects and to Old Charlie, who lies on his back, awake. The whites of his eyes shine like miniature lightbulbs as he stares unblinkingly at the ceiling. He turns his head and looks over at the lumpish form of Vera, lying completely covered by a tumble of blankets and sheets. He coughs lightly, uncoils, and rolls to his left into a sitting position, settling his feet into slippers at the side of his bed in a well-practiced routine. The mattress rises as he climbs out of bed. It takes a couple of seconds for Old Charlie to get acclimated, but in short fashion he finds his way out of his bedroom and descends the stairs. When his body weight lands on the third stair, a loud creaking noise stops his progress. He waits for a second, and not hearing anything from his bedroom, he continues down the stairs.

Old Charlie walks through the kitchen, and from a hook on the back of the door leading to the breezeway, he pulls on a well-worn pair of jeans and a thick flannel shirt over his pajamas. He puts on his winter coat, hat, and boots. Gingerly, he slips on his gloves, which are tight because of the bulky bandage on his left hand. He flicks on the outside garage light and slowly walks outside, the cold air slapping him fully awake. He looks at the streetlight at the corner of his property, and the sidewalk, a few errant snowflakes drifting at an angle, the last few soldiers leaving the battlefield as the storm moves on to the South. Twice he looks up and down the street, marveling at how new the world looks after a fresh snowfall. He sees the main road at the mouth of his cul-de-sac has been plowed.

Walking around the corner of the garage, he enters it from the side door. In the dark, he stretches his right hand toward the ceiling and fishes for a string he knows is there, a familiar lifeline in the black abyss. He finds and pulls it, firing up a forty-watt bulb hanging from the ceiling. Looking over the clutter of a small storage area, he starts rummaging through dusty boxes and wicker baskets that clutter the small alcove in front of his Chevy 4 x 4. Behind a box of Christmas ornaments, a bag of grass seed, and a crumpled box of gardening tools and supplies, he finds what he's seeking, a Flexible Flyer sled. It is at least forty years old. Lifting it out from behind its cardboard prison, Charlie sets it down on the cement floor to look it over. Cobwebs are interlaced throughout the undercarriage of the sled, and the carcass of the past season's resident spider shakes with the movement next to the egg sac of next season's brood. He dusts it off with a glove. Picking it back up with an apparent reverence, he lifts it up over the bed of his white pickup truck and sets it gently down.

After opening the automatic garage door with a button near the side door, Old Charlie gets in the truck and backs out of the garage slowly, gauging the driveway for slipperiness. Although he feels traction, he nonetheless slips the car into four-wheel drive and carefully finishes backing out onto the street. He keeps the lights off, just in case Vera happens to wake and look out the window. As he turns the corner, he stops the car and looks back at the house, focusing on his bedroom window. After a couple of deep breaths, he lightly removes his foot from the brake and his car rolls away. As soon as he is some distance from the house, he quickens the pace of the car. He doesn't see any other cars on the road except for an occasional plow. The oncoming truck flashes Old Charlie with its lights. As if for only a second, a feeling of panic overtakes him, but then he realizes it was just a signal for him to put his lights on, which he does. The sky is clearing rapidly now. Nor'easters come on quickly and they depart quickly.

Old Charlie drives in silence for a while, and then decides to turn on the radio. Though the car is equipped with a CD player, he and Vera only listen to talk radio or oldies in the car. Frank Sinatra is singing one of his favorites, "Fly Me to the Moon." He starts to hum along and leans back in his seat, feeling at peace. Without using his directional signal, he slows down and turns onto Mystic Street. As he nears his destination, Old Charlie turns his truck's lights down to their parking light setting, and lowers the radio to a whisper. He pulls to the side of the road by the Winchester Country Club's parking lot entrance. In addition to being a much-liked and often-used course, it turns into a popular sledding place for locals during the winter. He gets out and starts the long slog uphill to the crest.

A dog from the neighborhood hears—or smells—Charlie, and exits the comfort of her home through a doggie door. The dog stops abruptly at his electric fence, a nemesis remembered, denoted by squat, little flags around the yard's perimeter. The flags are barely visible, as the snowdrifts have just about covered their tips. The dog sees Old Charlie walking slowly up the hill. Tentatively she leans her head forward, nearing one of the flags, but stops and quickly recoils with a quiet yelp after hearing the humming sound that is coming from her electric-fence collar. The dog dances a small nervous jig as she again edges closer to the fence. Tilting forward as if pushed to do so by some unseen hand, she crosses the invisible line and is again driven back with a yelp.

The dog looks up toward the hill where she can hear Old Charlie coughing in the distance. Old Charlie has just about reached the halfway point of the hill, a plateau about as wide as a man is tall. The dog walks back from the fence, which is about twenty feet from where she stands. Barking once, as if to steel herself for what she is about to do, she leans back on her hindquarters and explodes into action, reaching full speed in a couple of seconds. Nearing the fence, she thrusts her hind legs downward one at a time into the snow, and stretching her front legs as far forward as they can stretch before take-off, finds enough traction and purchase to leap and clear the unseen line. Once she has crossed, she stops, looks back at her yard, wagging her tail as if contemplating her great deed. Old Charlie's coughing regains the dog's attention and she heads off to find its source. Old Charlie is at the hill's plateau. The dog now lets out a single, loud, authoritative bark, seemingly directed at Old Charlie.

The old man turns toward the sound and he squints his eyes. His knees lock and he becomes motionless, unable to move as this black torpedo of a dog races in his direction. As the dog approaches, Old Charlie tilts the sled upward and out at the speeding dog, like a shield to defend himself. The dog's torrid pace morphs slowly by degrees into an elegant prance, and she begins to circle Charlie, wagging her upturned tail excitedly. At first, Old Charlie keeps the sled between the two of them, but he slowly lowers his makeshift wall as he realizes the dog means no harm. He reaches down to pat the dog. The rope from the sled lies in the snow, and the dog grabs it in her mouth and drops it directly onto Charlie's boot. The dog takes a seat facing Charlie, and looks at the rope as if it were a living thing she was charged with guarding. Again, she picks up the rope with her mouth and drops it at Charlie's feet. This continues a couple more times.

"OK, girl. Is that why you're here? You want to go sledding? Well, that's why I'm here, too," says Old Charlie. "What's your name, pal?" Old Charlie bends down to get a closer look at the dog's collar. "Let me look at your tag. Well, it says here your name is Midnight. I guess you showed up at the right time, huh? It's almost twelve o'clock now. Glad to make your acquaintance, Midnight." Midnight lets out a single bark. "I take it you're here for a reason, too, huh?" continues Old Charlie. Midnight prances about like a thoroughbred horse at the starting gate before a big race. Old Charlie looks down at her, smiles, and pats her on the head. Midnight leans her body into Charlie's legs, rubbing along one side, then the other. "Thanks for the hugs, girlie."

There is some commotion at the periphery of Angie's dream, which is her current reality. As if on some synchronous cue, Old Charlie looks down the long sloping fairway of the golf course, the same direction in which Angie noticed some indistinct action. Even in her sleep, she realizes this is weird, as if she is dreaming for two.

In the distance, Charlie sees some four-legged figures, positioned in a cluster, looking up the hill in his direction. "What in God's name is that?" he says to himself. The group of animals—spindly, top-heavy black outlines against the bluish snow—start to move slowly in Old Charlie's direction. "Well, I'll be damned," he mutters under his breath.

Suddenly, Old Charlie's attention is taken from this downhill apparition, and his neck snaps involuntarily toward a stand of white pines on his right, slightly uphill. Wedges of light snow from the bottom branches of the tall evergreens drop in wet clumps as a pack of coyotes, five in number, push through the underbrush. Midnight's ears stand at attention and her tail drops between her legs like a magnet drawn south. At first, Midnight snarls, then deepens her voice into a growl. She falls silent, her demeanor eases, and her tail pops up like a flag waving in a parade. The coyotes trot toward the old man and the dog, high stepping and throwing their heads as if laughing uproariously, displaying their furry throats, making a show of expressing their vulnerability. As they near Old Charlie and Midnight, they lie down and thrust their legs toward the sky, playfully pawing the air, wiggling like worms caught aboveground in daylight. They make high-pitched, mewling sounds, as if trying to describe their joy.

Blinking his eyes in stunned amazement and frozen in place, Old Charlie barely notices as a line of deer, no longer mere apparitions from afar, advances up the hill to surround him, Midnight, and the frolicking pack of coyotes. The deer herd, split into two groups of five, begins to weave a complicated encirclement of the three creatures in the middle, promenading around them, moving in opposite directions. The entire tableau resembles a living merry-go-round. In the middle of it all, Old Charlie stands still in a modified defensive posture, tightly crouched at the knees, arms held chest high, with hands clenched into fists and elbows pointed outward at forty-five-degree angles, an NFL lineman protecting his quarterback. Midnight begins to chase her own tail next to him.

Then they all stop at once in unison, as if bidden to do so by a whistle with a frequency outside of human range. For a full minute, the only signs of life are the steaming breaths puffing into the crisp night air. Except for Charlie, who's holding his breath. The only species capable of complicated thought is completely unsure of what's going on. The entire assemblage has turned its rapt attention to Old Charlie, and the animals are all facing him, hyper alert in the way only animals can be, every single one looking him straight in the eyes as if expecting a speech. Old Charlie begins to breathe again, and his mouth curls into a huge smile. He begins to laugh silently to himself and then aloud, relinquishing control. He laughs long and hard, huge racking hoots and roars that allow a seemingly bottomless well of tears to be pumped from his tear ducts. Years of pent-up worries, concerns, and burdens get rinsed away like mud off a child's slide. Finally, his laughter begins to wind down and he gathers himself, with an occasional honking snigger escaping as he catches his breath.

He begins to stand up straighter and straighter, spine uncoiling and muscles loosening. He looks and feels more lithe and limber than he has in several decades.

The animals maintain their focus on him, and as one, they drop their forelegs in that universal expression of play. They surround him, some nudging him gently with their muzzles as he strokes as many as he can reach out to touch. After this getting-to-know-you period winds down, Old Charlie feels compelled to address his new-found friends.

"Well, well, well. I never would've expected this. How are we all? We have our own private little club, huh? Hey, I promise not to tell if you don't," he says with a laugh. Midnight stands apart from the others, and moves next to the sled. Old Charlie looks in her direction, but he can't help but resume patting and petting the deer and coyotes, clearly enjoying himself. Midnight barks, two short bursts, to get the old man's attention. She pokes her muzzle into the snow and scoops up the rope to the Flexible Flyer.

"Okay, girl," says Old Charlie to the black dog. He looks around at the expectant crowd of animals, and, using the tone of a carnival-ride barker, exclaims, "Okey-doke, folks. Let's saddle up and ride, boys and girls!" Under his breath he whispers, "I don't expect to slide much on this fresh surface with this old sled, but darn it, this whole night is crazy. Let's give it a go, shall we?" Flanked by the deer and the coyotes, the old man sets the old sled at the lip of the hilltop, plops himself tummy down on the Flexible Flyer, and grips *the steering handles, pushing them back and forth several times to loosen them up. He lifts his booted feet a little off the ground, as if in presentation at an exhibit. The lead coyote—the alpha male—and Midnight step behind him, place the top part of their heads to the soles of Old Charlie's feet, and push.*

"Whoooo hoooo! Yeeee-haw!" says Charlie as he begins to glide. In unison, they all speed down the slope. Exhilarated, the entire crew pauses at the base of the hill, catch their breath, and start back up as fast as their four legs—except for Charlie's two—can take them. They repeat their ride, over and over. After one of the downhill runs, during which Charlie slips off the sled near the bottom of the hill to fall facedown in the snow, he stops and reflects on what's happening all around him, and takes stock of his physical well-being. He flexes his bandaged hand and is amazed to discover that it no longer hurts. In fact, nothing hurts; he feels none of the accustomed aches and pains that have accumulated over the years. Back? Great! Knees? Check!

Just as he begins to ruminate over this development, he becomes aware of the fact his glasses have fallen off. "What the heck?" he whispers under his breath. "I can see clear as day! Twenty-twenty with no glasses!" Eyes drawn back to his hand, he unpeels his gloves and unwraps the still-bloody bandage. The cut is gone, just smooth skin, ivory in the moonlight. "Well, I'll be damned." He looks up, sees the animals again gathered around, and says, "Okay! Just a few more runs, eh? Last one up's a monkey's uncle! Oops, I guess that would have to be me. I'm the closest relative to a monkey here!" He chortles at his own joke and they all go up the hill.

Old Charlie and his team of friends sled down the hill countless times, tireless and overflowing with the joy of living. They go back up the hill after each run just as fast as they did the first time. Again and again through the night, they sled. Nearly three hours have gone by when Old Charlie stops and drops to a knee, then rolls over onto his side to rest—just for a little bit, he says to himself. He stays on his side for about ten minutes, caught in the moment as he half-hugs the sled as if it were a sleeping child. The old man lies still for a while, breathing shallowly. He feels inexplicably warmer now, and more at peace than he has in a long, long time, more than he thought was even possible. The cooling snow sends a light mist heavenward, creating a halo around the moon, a wafer well into its descent toward Earth. With a resigned sigh, he gets up and starts walking uphill one more time.

He is almost at the top of the hill when he hesitates and turns his head to look skyward. Midnight and the rest of the gang sit motionless around him. At first Old Charlie's face becomes solemn. The animals all lie down and their heads point down, as if bowing. He takes off his ski hat to rub his sweating brow. A small twist of steam rises from his head and briefly floats aloft before disappearing into the night sky. It collects and spirals above Old Charlie's head and gains strength as it rises into the heavens. He watches with amazement, as if he could see beyond the limits of the human eye.

He sees the stars in sharp focus. They appear within reach, and he thinks he's able to see more deeply into the sky than ever before. The animals have drawn back a bit, giving him a respectful berth, but standing still as statues, attendants at a solitary crèche.

Midnight's head tilts to the side. Her tail, which has been in full swing the entire evening, lies motionless. Her large dark brown eyes are fixed on the steam spiraling upward, and she behaves as if she is watching her master. Old Charlie's expression brightens and his eyes begin to tear up. He has the largest of smiles and looks as if he is being spoken to. His four-legged friends drift off into the woods, Midnight heads home, and Charlie just stands there, sled at his feet, looking toward the celestial streams of light, and at a lone male silhouette in the middle of it at the top of the hill.

CHAPTER 11

Giddy Up

The dream fades to wakefulness and Angie gathers her senses slowly, a bee emerging from entrapment in watered honey. She uncoils her body out of a fetal curl as her mind struggles to get its bearing. She sees her bedroom wall, and recognizes the old Backstreet Boys poster she could never quite bear to take down. She raises her head and sees her bed's headboard, several hats—a pink Red Sox one and a black cap with its insignia obscured by the overlapping pink one on the left bedpost—reassure her she is safe in her childhood home.

Whoa, that was the weirdest dream, she thinks, still unsure whether it was a good one or a bad one. *It was as if I was watching that old man do stuff, yet I was seeing what he saw while he was doing it, and I was seeing it all through his eyes. Like I was watching him have a dream within a dream that I'm dreaming. Wait. That old man was Charlie Fife,* she realizes with a start. *Geez, talk about participatory journalism!*

Angie raises her body into a sitting position, and tries to trap the details of her dream in her mind before she gives herself over to reality. *Okay, what did it mean? What happened? Remember, girl, remember.* She strains to grasp the reins before its clarity is lost. *Okay, dancing with the wolves…okay, not wolves… check. Snow, check. Sledding, check. What did he see? Stars, a bandage over a wound that was just a faded line—check. Oh, wait, wound—uncheck. What wound? There wasn't any mention of a wound in the police report. Okay, what else? Ah! A silhouette by a setting moon. Places time way past midnight…the silhouette. The silhouette. It looked familiar. But from where? I know that posture, I know that posture. But how do I know it? How?*

After five or so minutes of trying to summon the real-life person to flesh out the silhouette from her dream, she gets up, stretches, and heads downstairs, where she hears noises and conversation. She gets to the kitchen door, and watches a routine unfold that is part of her family's regular evening dance. An olive green dog dish, six inches in diameter, finishes its final revolution like a spinning top before rattling to a stop on the hardwood kitchen floor. Cliff smirks as Daisy patiently waits for the theatrics to stop, and begins snatching up the mixture of hard kibble, cubes of boiled chicken, and mashed sweet potato. Daisy crunches on the kibble, picking her head up ever so slightly, looking at Cliff as if to get his approval.

"Why can't you simply place her food down like a normal person? Spinning it like that drives her crazy, you know," says Sue as she applies the final touches to Angie's favorite dish, shrimp scampi. Cliff stands guard over Daisy, with his arms crossed, slowly shaking his head.

"When you make another batch of Ms. Daisy's special mixture, can you please put some of it aside for yours truly?" asks Cliff in a monotone voice. Sue tries to hold herself from laughing as she carries a pot of boiling water and spaghetti to the sink to drain. She purposely refuses to look at Cliff, afraid she'll laugh and spill the scolding water everywhere. She rushes her final steps to unload the heavy pot into its matching strainer resting in the white, cast-iron double sink. A backdraft of steam flushes around her head and she turns to avoid the blast of heat.

"Did you hear what Daddy said, Angie? He wants me to prepare some of Daisy's dog food for him." Cliff moves near Sue, trying to tickle her, playful and at the same defending his honor.

Angie lingers by the side of the stove, reaches delicately into the pan to grab a single sautéing shrimp by its tail, placing her other hand under it to prevent any drops of butter, garlic, and olive oil from hitting the floor. She slides by Sue and bites into the shrimp over the sink.

"Awethome, Mom," she says around a mouthful of food. "I jutht hadda nithe nap."

"Well, you must have been tired, sweetie. I can' remember the last time you took a nap," says Sue as she checks on the remaining shrimp. "We are about two minutes away from dinner. Cliff, can you please put the bread and hot pepper on the table?"

"Is Dad going to eat what we're eating, or is he going to get down on the floor and eat Daisy's stuff?" Sue laughs at the mother-and-daughter moment achieved at the expense of their favorite male.

"I'm so glad you're home, sweetie," says Sue, "for whatever reason."

"Me, too," says Cliff from the dining room. "Who knows what we'd be eating if you weren't here?"

The threesome sit in the octagon-shaped dining room, just off the kitchen. They eat without speaking for a while, and then Cliff breaks the companionable silence. "Our little girl is growing up, Sue." Angie has a smile, feeling a sense that the storm has passed.

"How's the project?" Cliff asks, then impatiently speaks again before getting a response. "You need to be mindful of any research you're doing on this thing. I'm sure Mr. Armstrong explained that to you?"

"Yeah, but…we went over all this stuff yesterday, Dad. And yes, I met with Mr. Armstrong, and the most dangerous thing I've done so far is walk around a golf course off-season, which is probably the safest time to do so, what with the lack of flying golf balls." She feels a slight pang at leaving out the mystery texts and the strange dream, but knows bringing them up would curb her activities as surely as if she says she just met a fellow named Jeffrey Dahmer, and he seemed a pretty safe date for her school's Spring Fling. She waits, forcing her father to pick up the conversational thread.

Seeming slightly preoccupied, Cliff plays with his fork, turning it over in circles between his thumb and forefinger. Angie recognizes her father's distracted pause as his way of pushing his pensiveness aside and summoning the perfect phrasing for what he wants to say.

"You know, this all has me thinking," he finally says, the preamble setting the tone that he's about to say something meaningful. "The passing of loved ones, the challenges a sick kid like Chas has, or the girl you talked about up in Syracuse. Really, any tragedy or hardship. Marcie. Her family. You know, after she died, they just crumbled. Her parents stayed together, they stayed in their house, as you know, but they never really *lived* in it again. Just kind of walked around like ghosts, haunted. Didn't want help. They've never been rude or anything, they just kind of came and went like broken spirits. Saddest thing you can imagine. For everybody, including you, honey. You watched Marcie suffer, and that caused you suffering, and we suffered right along with you." His voice begins to crack, his eyes fill, and he makes no attempt to hide his tears.

Angie is taken back by her dad's emotion. She thinks of what Bill Armstrong had taught her about asking the second why.

"Dad, why are you telling me this?"

Cliff stops eating, leans back in his chair, and rubs his temple.

"You know, I'm not sure exactly. I guess the details of everything we've been hearing just brings up some stuff from the past," he says as he looks toward Sue, who is listening, sipping her wine and watching him over the rim of her glass.

"What kind of stuff?" asks Angie.

"A family that has a disabled child, well, they are disabled, too. Disabled by proxy is the way I think of it. I just know you need to be sensitive to this if you plan on sniffing around some of these people in the middle of their…hardships."

Angie remains still, hoping her dad will continue. In all her years, she has never seen him so demonstrative about the topic of sick kids. Angie remembers what Bill Armstrong had told her and remains quiet, not offering to say a word. Cliff breaks the silence.

"I know what I'm talking about," he continues firmly. Angie tries to remain still, but feels she needs to provide an empathetic sign, so she nods her head, a subtle assent.

"I was a disabled kid, you know," he says, knowing his words will catch Angie by surprise, but wanting to wade into the waters slowly. "I was a sick kid, pretty seriously sick for a pretty long time, a long time ago." He stops to let this sink in.

"What?" Incredulous, Angie searches for some words, some foundation to grab on to as she feels her reality shifting. *This is some game*, she thinks. *Maybe this is some bizarre reality TV show called* Shock Your Kid into Spontaneous Seizures *and somebody's gonna come out of the closet with a camera and we can all go back to a nice glass of wine and some dessert.* She jumps back into the rising waters. "What happened, Dad? What do you mean, disabled?"

"Well, I had cancer as a child," Cliff says quietly. Angie's eyes switch from him to Sue.

"Mom, did you know this?" There are other questions. She wants to know if she has been isolated in her ignorance, kept apart from some profoundly important truth.

Sue nods, doesn't say anything.

"O-kay," says Angie slowly, letting the news sink in. "So…I am like the only one here without a clue as to what's true.

Basic, important family history: Dad had cancer. Daughter's need to know this important—vitally important—fact? Zero. Right. Any other bombshells now that we're playing the new game show *Let's Spill the Family's Beans*? I mean, c'mon, what the…" She stops herself short of cursing, aware that pulling that needless punch will keep her on higher ground. She sniffles, catches herself. She is too hurt—and too proud—to let down her guard. But after looking out the kitchen window into the dark for a full minute, and then back at her dad, she relents. "I mean, why didn't anyone tell me? You've kept this secret all this time. I don't get it. Why?" She slaps the table once, emphatically.

Sue reaches out her left hand to encircle Angie's. Angie turns her hand palm side up and opens it. They clasp, squeeze once, and hang on tight.

"It was probably more my fault we didn't say anything to you, Angie," says Sue. "We watched what you went through with Marcie getting sick and then…dying. The right time just never seemed right. We—I—just thought you had already been through so much when you were so young, and that…"

Cliff sees his wife struggling and picks up the thread. "You see, Ange, you had such a bad time of it when Marcie had cancer, and it never seemed like it was the right time to say anything. To be truthful, I'm surprised I told you even now. You can call it parental intuition, or overprotectiveness, or whatever. We didn't want you to think cancer was everywhere and that it was this...huge specter that hangs over our lives all the time. It's there, sure, but it doesn't have to be an 'it' with a capital 'I.' Life is a full, wonderful adventure, and we didn't want you to carry around knowledge of this disease like this huge burden on your shoulder, like some ponderous, bloodthirsty vulture."

"Dad, I'm glad you did tell me. You know, you're right. I guess that life is an open road and all that, but can we leave the carnivore vultures out? I get it—you didn't want me to fear something I had no control over. Fine. Thanks. You sure waited long enough, but...whatever. You owe me details, all of them. Start to finish and whatever lies ahead."

"Fair enough, honey," says Cliff. The tension has been lifted and he prepares himself to tell her his story. "Why now? I don't know. Just seems like with everything going on with you in your world, and with you talking about Marcie to your mom again last night, that this was a good time." He pauses. Angie waits, putting on a mask of impassivity, keeping herself perfectly still.

"I first got sick when I was five," Cliff begins, sounding like someone recounting his story at a twelve-step meeting. "It started innocuously with a whole cluster of nosebleeds, if something with a name like acute lymphocytic leukemia can share a sentence with the word 'innocuous.'"

He smiles a tight-lipped smile and continues. "I got really tired really easily, and my bones ached like a bad flu. Except the flu didn't go away. Finally Gramma and Gramps took me in for tests. I'll never forget that. Doctor Bates was his name. He was a GP, back when there was such a thing as general practitioners. He was a tall, skinny guy, bald with really big eyes behind these enormous Coke-bottle glasses, and this tiny, little mouth he kept open all the time in the shape of an 'o.' Looked like an alien. Never forgot this—he made me lie down on the examining table, on top of that really thin paper, and he was feeling my stomach, my liver, spleen. He didn't say anything while he was doing it, but the second time he squeezed my left side under my ribs, it hurt like heck and I lurched a little bit. 'That hurt?' he asked me. He knew. Just gave me a pat on the knee and told me I could get dressed. I was just a kid, but I knew something was really wrong."

Angie, spellbound, swallows, her mouth suddenly very dry. She realizes she hasn't drawn a breath in a while. "Go on, Dad. Then what?"

"Well, then it was a blur of tests, more tests, and then when I got tired of the tests, they ran some more tests. I was pulled out of school, although they brought me schoolwork to do at home, and at first some kids came over and we played. Then I began to get chemo, which made me more tired, and when kids came over to play, I pretty much just watched them play. As I sat isolated inside the house, I remember getting mad whenever they'd be outside just sitting around not doing anything. 'Why aren't they doing anything?' I'd ask your grandmother. I couldn't understand why anyone who *could* play would ever want to stop playing.

"Finally, as the chemo dragged on and I got more and more tired and I lost all my hair, the kids stopped coming over. Gramma would play board games and read to me. Gramps would, too. It just about killed them to have to see me like that, but they tried to never let on how much it hurt to see it. I'd glance over at one of them sometimes while I was reading or watching TV, and catch them watching me with a look as if their hearts were breaking. And they were. Late night, if I couldn't sleep and went to the fridge for a glass of milk, it wasn't uncommon to catch Gramps just silently sitting in that rocker. That whole winter was so boring and I couldn't understand what had happened, and why I was yanked out of my regular life like a fly caught by a kid and thrown in a jar.

"By that spring, it was as if I was still that fly, but the air was running out and all I wanted to do was lie down and do nothing at all, except be carried into the hospital for the radiation phase of my treatment. At times, I scared myself. Gramps, carrying me, would pass a mirror, and I'd lurch and tighten at the sight of what I had become. Yellow skin just covering a skeleton, eyes bloodshot, set back with dark circles. As you know, sometimes to cure you, they almost have to kill you. I felt really sorry for myself, and that is the probably the worst feeling a little boy—or girl—can feel. Almost worse than knowing you might die before you learn how to tie a knot on your sneakers, or ride a bike without training wheels."

Angie is getting a little caught up in the emotion, even though her father's sitting there has given away the story's ending as being somewhat along the lines of "and they lived happily ever after." As her father takes a sip of coffee, she offers a serving of sympathy. "Wow, Dad, I am *so* sorry you had to go through that."

"It's okay, honey. Everything happens for a reason. Going through what I did made me the great guy and wonderful father you see sitting before you today," he says, lightly self-mocking, grinning.

"Anyway, I got a break from the fly jar for a few weeks that following summer, just before my final round of chemo. Gramma and Gramps sent me to a summer camp for children going through the same kind of thing I was. Got to be outside, well, almost *forced* to be outside," he laughs quietly to himself. "They treated us more like ranch hands than sick kids. We had to clean stables, rake hay, feed and water horses, kind of like the Don Imus ranch that kids enjoy today. We got to ride horses and swim in the pond near the bunk-house, sure, but only after we did our chores as best as we could. They worked us hard, and we played hard, too. Just like real kids. Normal kids. For most of us, it was the best thing that could've happened. It was for me, that's for sure. To be normal and not have everybody looking at you as if they're about to cry, or worse, do everything but breathe for you. The pity that gets heaped on you is almost worse than the radiation. There was no pity for us at Pegasus Camp, I can tell you that. Love, yes, plenty of that. And freedom. Freedom to be just a kid, not a sick kid."

Cliff goes silent, swept up in an outgoing tide taking him back to his childhood. Angie and Sue sit, letting him drift as they reflect on the story.

"Hey!" he says. "You want to see some pictures of the camp? It was out in Kalispell, Montana. The place I got my life back from? They're in a box upstairs in my desk. Hey, there, cub reporter, I'm surprised you never snooped around and saw them for yourself." His method of breaking off an emotional moment by joking around is well known in the Clarke household.

"Yeah, Dad, I'd love to see them," Angie says, unwilling to break from the seriousness of what she's just heard, as if to do so would lessen the sanctity of this new information.

"Be right back," Cliff says, as he gets up and goes upstairs. Angie and Sue look at each other. Both look down and realize they are still holding hands across the table. Sue breaks the contact and gets up. "I've seen the photos, Ange. You look at them with your father while I clean up." Angie, left alone, folds her arms over each other and waits. Breathes a light, muffled "phew."

Cliff comes back into the room with an old faded pink Macy's box, takes the top off, and, pulling his chair over next to Angie, sits down. He takes out a heap, the photos fanning out in his hand like cards, and plops them down on the table. He idly picks through them while Angie lets him do his sifting work, a miner panning for memories.

"Here's one. Happy birthday to me." Wry. Deflecting emotions recalled.

Angie takes the photograph from Cliff. A pale boy, eyes huge in the middle of dark circles that would make Alice Cooper proud, with a birthday cone hat perched off-center on top of a bald head. The boy is trying to smile. Failing.

"Jeez. Oh, my God, Dad," Angie whispers. Chokes out a small cough that kick-starts a sob, then tears.

"Hey," Cliff says quietly. "The boy lives. See?" He pinches his forearm. "I'm showing this so you have the whole story. The *his*-story. You want to stop?"

"No, Dad, I don't want to stop. Just…you know…"

"Yup, I know. Here's another, a little more cheery." The same little boy, bundled in a parka with the hood up that looks as if it has swallowed the boy whole, is sitting on a bench on a full-size wagon hitched to a huge horse with blinders on. "That's Gramma," he says, pointing at the horse. "She was a tough old thing back in the day. Probably 'cause she ate like a horse."

"Dad."

"Here's one of the Pegasus." He passes her a photo of a large log cabin, belted by a wraparound porch with Adirondack chairs lined up its entire length. Almost every one has either a saddle, a horse blanket, or a beach towel in it. There are a number of wheelchairs amidst them, with IV tubes slung alongside. Trees stand sentinel in a half circle around the cabin. But what really captures the camera's attention is a group of children, clad in buckskin, jeans, and cowboy hats. The fact none of the kids has any hair curling out from the sides of their hats doesn't detract from the joy each one shows in the form of smiles plastered across their faces. Each child could light up a city with the light pouring out of his beaming eyes. "I'm the last one on the right, first row. Next to the counselor, right there." Cliff taps the child next to a tall black man. "Toothy, aren't I?" he asks.

Angie feels her blood freeze in the back of her neck, her equilibrium wobble, and her arms go dead. She feels an immediate rush of blood as she recognizes the man in the photograph. "Wait," she croaks, stopping Cliff from dropping the photo back in its box, clamping his wrist like a cop stopping a pickpocket.

Startled, he looks at her, puzzled by her forceful, adamant reaction. "All right, Ange, no need to get violent."

"Who is this guy next to you?" She taps the man next to the boy he just tapped in the photo.

"Um, that's, uh…a man named Michael," Cliff says, a little unsure of his answer, as he is of the reason for the question that necessitated it.

"Who was he, though? What did he do at the camp?" she unfolds the questions, urgent.

"Like I said, he was a counselor. I remember him also being a nurse. Great guy. Got us up in the saddle with him while we fixed fences and gave us horseback riding lessons. Taught me how to swim."

"Where is he now?" Angie demands.

"Honey, he's probably, like, in Florida, playing golf or something. Maybe volunteering with intubations in some rest home, where he would no doubt be living by now. I mean, he would have to be at least seventy or so."

"He's not seventy," Angie says, more to herself than to her father.

"Angie, neither one of us is any good at math, but even I can do this one. Let's see—forty-five plus, say, thirty is…uh, help me out here, uh…I know!" He snaps his fingers. "It's seventy-five."

"Dad, I just saw him a few days ago. In Syracuse. He was the guy with the little girl in the wheelchair. The one who winked at me, same time she did."

"That's crazy. Maybe it's his son or something. Can't be the same guy."

"Dad, it is." Right then, it hits her—she knows the profile, too. It's the silhouette from her dream. *Mine and Old Charlie's,* she thinks, amending her thought. She blinks, opens her mouth, and quickly turns away from her father, hiding this revelation. *No way he'll believe this one. As Mr. Armstrong would say, keep your own counsel.*

Shifting gears back to a line of questioning she can control, she asks, "What was this Michael guy's last name?"

"Ange, I don't know. All I can remember is we called him Michael. That's what he insisted we call him."

"What else can you tell me about him?"

"Well, he took a special interest in all of us kids. It wasn't like this was just a job for him. I remember that."

"Did you stay in touch after? You know, when you left the camp and went home?"

"No..." he answers, thinking, straining to recollect. "He left before I did. It was about the same time as this guy here," he says, pointing to another smiling boy in the photo. "I know he was sent home with this kid because his grandfather wasn't well and someone needed to accompany him on the plane." He stops and thinks. "Him, I do know. Name's Eli Cohen. Became a doctor. Ran into him at some fundraiser we were both at about ten years ago, and we remembered each other's names from the guest list. He became an oncologist. I'm sure you don't need a psychology degree to figure that one out."

"Okay, Dad. Where's he, then?"

"Well, last I knew, he was in charge of a pediatrics wing down in Providence, Rhode Island. Worked at the hospital started by the toy people, Hasbro. Hasbro Children's Hospital. Don't know if he's still there, but I'm sure you could find that out."

"I'm going to start with him."

"Okay. Start as in start what?

"I need to track this Michael guy."

Cliff, convinced his daughter has made a case of mistaken identity, but equally aware it would be fruitless to try to dissuade her, nods. "Get ready to find some wrinkled, stooped over, ex-camp counselor, unless this is some father-son combo who's made murdering elderly people into some sort of family business." He laughs. "But I still think your winker man just has a passing resemblance to some guy who made it his life's calling to help kids through a rough patch in their lives."

"Dad, I'm going down there tomorrow. To Providence. This is a lead, and I'm going to see where it takes me. It could break the whole thing wide open."

"All right, Angie. But this is your last shot in this game, and then it's back to school. I'd rather watch you get your diploma with a bunch of other parents outside in a procession, as opposed to seeing it mailed to you next winter. Deal?"

"Deal."

"Okay, then. What do you say we go help your mother finish up in the kitchen? With any luck, we'll be just in time to have to do nothing."

"I know, Dad, and look good doing it."

CHAPTER 12

Tomorrow's Light

Angie beats the alarm clock awake the next morning and turns it off before it can say a thing. Having spent the last hour and a half trying to get back to sleep, she doesn't want to grant it the final word after a long, mostly sleepless night. *Of course it didn't help I Googled Michael + camp counselor + children and clicked through about a thousand of the fifteen and a half million hits,* she thinks. *But I sure learned a lot about Hasbro, Dr. Cohen, and childhood cancer.* "And," she says, "I got a phone number."

Getting showered and dressed—black pants suit; pink Oxford shirt; knee-high, dark brown boots; and small, hoop earrings—with the speed to which she has become accustomed as someone with early morning classes, Angie gets downstairs just in time to say good-bye to her parents. Her father has class at eight and her mother goes to the gym before her stint at the library. Making herself some toast and pouring herself some coffee, she takes a seat at the table with her backpack and some crackers, a notebook, and two pens (in case one runs dry; she's learned *that* lesson). She then takes the photo of her father, the camp, and Michael out of her pocketbook to look at it again. "Nope. I am *not* crazy. This *is* the same guy. Or they have made unreported gains in cloning and the one I saw is a clone."

Glancing at the clock, Angie sees it's eight, and she gets her cell phone out to call the oncology department at Hasbro. Good luck graces her with a live person after several recorded options and prompts. She gives her name, says she is writing a story for the *Arlington Advocate* on adolescent cancers, drops her father's name, adding that he's a friend of Dr. Cohen's— pushing the envelope a tad—and asks for an appointment. After a short stay on the phone island called Hold, Dr. Cohen's receptionist comes back with surprising news, even for the optimist Angie considers herself to be: "Yes, Dr. Cohen can see you today at ten thirty."

She wants to give herself plenty of time—another lesson she will never forget when working a story—and so she heads for the vehicular Russian roulette that is the Route 128 corridor. She leaves the car radio and her iPod silenced so she can organize her thoughts and prepare the questions she has for the doctor. She ponders the differences between the cancers her father and the doctor had—with Michael around—and the motor-control diseases of Stephanie—again, with Michael—and Chas. *I'm still unclear about Michael's role in this one*, she thinks. Furthermore, she wonders whether or not these differences are important in the overall scheme of her story. This stirs her to think about Marcie, which provokes a random thought to ask *her* for help.

"Marcie, old friend," she says softly. "Just between us girls—can you maybe show me some sign I'm on the right track here, maybe lead me down the right path?" She looks around, reading license plates, looking for roadside signage that might break down to a sign from above.

Nothing. *Oh, well. Like they say, the answers to a prayer are either "yes," "no," or "wait." I'll wait.*

Having driven most of the way with her subconscious operating its own human version of cruise control and reflexes, Angie notices the Dudley Street exit she wants to take off I-95 is coming up. She finds the hospital's parking lot, parks her car in the upper level, and heads for the main building, noticing the stark difference between the new children's hospital and the long-standing Rhode Island Hospital buildings. Both sport similar shades of beige brick, but the adult hospital has accented dark brown metal framing, while the outlines of the children's building are lighter colors, pink and teal. Both buildings share the same rotating doorways facing each other, each one in a state of constantly spinning motion. The action at the main hospital seems to be heavier, and Angie wonders if there will be a time in the future when neither door would have to be spinning at all.

She's about halfway down the walkway to the entrance, almost even with a group of people in nursing and physician assistant uniforms huddled in small groups, smoking just outside the line delineated by a NO SMOKING sign. Just as she is stricken by the irony of health-care workers voluntarily working to not take care for their health, Maroon 5 summons her, muffled in her handbag. She stops, takes it out, expecting a check-in call from one of her parents, or—hope against hope—Jack, and unlocks the screen. It's a text: "GKTW." She turns the phone off and hurries it back into her bag.

Panicked, Angie wheels around to look for anyone looking at her. Which, of course, has the effect of actually causing people to look at her. She resumes her way inside, quickening her pace as she slithers through the rotating paddles of the vertical waterwheel.

Inside, Angie feels a little safer, a little less exposed. Her rational mind overrides her wishful thinking, however, and she comes to the unwelcome realization that the texter could be *inside* the building. Or still outside, waiting. Or three thousand miles away, sitting on a Malibu beach having some bicoastal fun at her expense. Brought out of her fearful reverie by the stream of people being spit out of the doorway to surge on either side of her, Angie shelves the texting mystery and steps to the oval information desk. Two large Norman Rockwell-style murals, depicting the hospital in present day and in the 1860s, are set behind red velveteen rope. Several gray-haired women behind it look at her, expectantly.

"Help you, dear?" asks one who bears an uncanny resemblance to Betty White—diminutive, hair teased just so, with a pair of reading glasses dangling over a light yellow camelhair cardigan. *Maybe it's the cheery attitude*, thinks Angie.

"I'm looking for Dr. Eli Cohen's office," she answers. "I have an appointment." She blushes slightly, aware she's overcompensating to allow for the differences in stature between herself, little Angie Clarke, and the renowned oncologist and Harvard professor she is requesting to see. She clears her throat and raises an eyebrow at the women, trying to recapture stature lost.

"Sure, dear," says the Betty White look-alike, unfazed by the weather changes drifting across Angie's face. "You are here," she says, pointing to a map on the back of a pamphlet. "You want to turn left behind this desk, and walk down the hallway through the Davol wing into the Hasbro Children's Hospital wing, and just past the dancing dolphins, take the elevator to the lower level. You'll see the pediatric offices there. They'll know where Dr. Cohen is. You'll know the dolphins when you see them." She laughs; it's an oft-told line.

"Thank you very much," says Angie, back in control as she collects the map and moves on her way. She alternates glancing at the map with carrying out their instructions, walking along corridors that are brightly lit thanks to an outside wall made entirely out of glass. On the opposite wall, also made of glass, are encased figurines, board games, movies, books, and toys from childhoods past and present: Play-Doh, SpongeBob SquarePants, Mr. Potato Head, *The Wizard of Oz*, and Rainbow Dash from the My Little Pony series, a doll she and Marcie spent hours with, combing its rainbow-hued mane. This makes her smile.

Just inside the entrance to the Hasbro Children's Hospital are the dancing dolphins, a detailed five-foot-tall glass sculpture of two playful dolphins dancing on the surface of the sea, noses pointing skyward. The décor summons an underwater world, comprised of tranquil blues and greens designed to ease the minds—and the fears—of the sick young people who have to go through the hospital's doors. Even the name of the sculpture, *Come Play with Me*, is designed to place a positive spin on the experiences the children will have to endure in order to, hopefully, one day walk away from the hospital for good, cured.

Spotting the bank of elevators referred to in the directions, Angie walks over to wait, and in doing so is joined by a little girl about seven years old accompanied by her parents. The girl is wearing a Red Sox hat; nothing but bare skin lies underneath. Angie smiles at her, and the little girl smiles back. She's holding a redheaded American Girl doll, the kind of doll that allows children to select one that matches their likeness in hair color. This causes Angie to wonder what it would be like if there were a bald-headed doll marketed for kids undergoing chemo, a dark thought she wishes she never had. She looks up at the parents, almost afraid they can read her thoughts, and notices the mother has red hair. She decides to take a chance, driven by intuition.

"That's an awfully pretty doll you have there," says Angie, squatting down to attain eye level with the little girl. "What's her name?" She's pretty sure what it's going to be, hopes she isn't being foolish by grasping at straws. She has to know, though, has to hear the little girl tell her the doll's name.

"Marcie," says the little girl. "Her name's Mar-cie," she says the name again, chopping up the syllables into a playful singsong. She moves the doll's head to point its mouth at Angie. "Marcie says hello."

Angie feels a rush of prickly warmth wash over her, from the back of her neck down her body. She feels a quick burst of emotion surge back up, as if it wants to pour back out as tears and sobs. But she applies the brakes, absorbs the emotion, accepts the depth of feeling, and allows it to inhabit her fully. She feels as if she could bench-press an elephant and run through a wall. Empowered. Whole. Connected.

Finding words as she stands up, Angie looks at the little girl and says softly, "I love your little friend. Great outfit, too."

"Thanks, lady," says the little girl.

The elevator dings and Angie sees the downward arrow is lit up. She moves to step on as the doors open, and, still bemused to have been called a lady at her still-tender age, looks back at the little girl, and says, "It was nice to meet you, young lady, and it was good to see you again, Marcie."

"We say good-bye!" says the little girl. "Maybe see you again!"

They part with a wave, as the door closes and Angie heads downward, the floor lurching, altering gravity for half a heartbeat. Thinking about the little girl, Angie feels as if she has been bestowed with steel to help her through what she knows will be an intimidating meeting, given the nature of her questions and the standing of the person to whom she will be asking them. No one on the elevator looks at one another; everyone has eyes on the floor indicator lights. It's elevator etiquette, heightened by the gravity of the situations of the people in this particular enclosed space. An adult female nurse attends one child in a wheelchair. Another child is being held by an adult, most likely the boy's father. The child's face is buried in his father's neck.

The doors open and the other occupants, allowing the child in the wheelchair to be wheeled out first, file out into the downstairs lobby. Angie, the last to leave, gets off and walks down the busy corridor per her directions, her leather soles clip-clopping on the immaculately clean tiled floor as she searches for, and finds, the signs for the Hematology/Oncology offices.

She references the diagram but goes down the wrong hallway by mistake. She realizes it, stops, spins around, and crashes into a man who has been traveling in the same direction, trailing behind her. The man, tall and clad in a freshly pressed white lab coat, has several charts inside of folders slip from his grasp and fall to the ground, where they glide to form a pile with Angie's bag and water bottle, which she has dropped. The man appears to be in his sixties, with a mane of white hair that matches a luxuriant moustache that curls up slightly at the ends. With a powder-blue dress shirt that accents bright blue eyes and charcoal gray pants, he gives off the appearance of easy elegance. Angie's eyes are drawn to his Sesame Street bow tie, and then to the insignia on his lab coat that reads "Chief of Pediatric Oncology, Eli Cohen, MD."

"Oh, heavens," says the man, before Angie can utter a word. "I'm sorry, young lady. Look what I've done. Are you OK?" asks Dr. Cohen. He and Angie scramble to pick up the mess before them.

"It was totally my fault. I'm so sorry. Really, I need to be looking where I'm going," replies Angie. Dr. Cohen lowers his hand to help Angie up from the tile. She grabs his hand and as her eyes travel upward. She reads his name again, only this time aloud.

"Dr. Cohen," says Angie. Dr. Cohen nods and smiles.

"Now you know who I am. Who might you be, young lady? Are you certain you are okay?"

Angie adjusts her clothes, making sure everything is in place. "Yes, I'm good. And *I'm* sorry. That was totally my fault. I was actually on my way to see you."

Dr. Cohen chuckles. "You certainly have a direct way of finding someone, don't you, Ms…?" He patiently looks at Angie and doesn't say a word, as he waits for her to complete his sentence.

"Oh, I'm sorry. Angie. I mean, Clarke. I mean, Angie Clarke." Angie swings her bag back over her shoulder and extends her hand to shake his.

"Oh, Cliff's daughter. Right. I see from having looked at my schedule that we'll be spending some time together this morning. Actually, could you walk with me, Angie? I'm a bit tardy and behind schedule this morning. Can we walk and talk, as they say? Would that be OK?"

"Oh, yeah, sure, sure," replies Angie. They continue in the direction in which Dr. Cohen was originally traveling.

Angie reaches into her backpack to retrieve the picture and extends it to Dr. Cohen. Talking ceases as Dr. Cohen extracts his specs from his lab coat's upper front pocket and puts them on, with them running down to the edge of his nose.

"Let's see. What have we here?"

His eyes first widen as if alarmed, and then twitch and refocus.

"Well, Angie, looks like you and your dad have been going through some old photos. How is Cliff?"

"He's great. He sends his best."

"He is an old friend. Just because we haven't spent a lot of time together over the past several decades or so doesn't mean he's not someone who isn't in my thoughts often—very often. We shared a very intense and important experience together a long time ago." He smiles again, more restrained and reflective this time, mustache barely moving while his eyebrows arch to crease his forehead with wrinkling lines.

His voice, softer now: "Sometimes a short, extraordinary time is a more potent memory than a long extended time of…shallower moments, shall we say."

Angie leans in toward Dr. Cohen, who turns toward her and holds out the photo so they both can see it.

Angie, caught up short by Dr. Cohen's apparent acceptance of her small subterfuge to gain a meeting with him, cannot think of a thing to say. She is not used to being at a loss for words. She finds herself just looking at this elegant man, hoping she can think of something—hopefully not too stupid—to say. Her eyes drift from his, down to his colorful bow tie. Nothing comes to mind for her to say. He hands her back the photo and, as if by reflex, she places it back in her bag.

"So you mentioned to Maria yesterday you were a reporter working on a story? Story on me?" He smiles, teasing. "Better yet, on what we do here at Hasbro?"

Not wanting to lie, but not wanting to blurt the exact truth, either, Angie hesitates before answering. "Well, yes, I would like to do a story on the…things you do here. Um, but I also have something else I want to ask you about."

"Really? What would that be?" He stops and half-turns to look at her, as foot traffic snakes past them on either side. He moves back against a wall and Angie moves next to him so people, most of whom are clad in rubber-soled shoes that squeak, can more easily get to where they are going. Everyone seems to have a purpose.

Angie reaches into her handbag and extracts the same photo that has given *her* a sense of purpose. She holds it out to him, he takes it again, and peers at it intently. "Hmm. Same photo? Yup, that's your dad and me, all right! That answer your question?" His eyebrows are raised and he grins at her cautiously, but not unkindly. He starts to hand the photograph back to her, but she neglects to take it from his grasp. He continues to hold it as his arm relaxes by his side.

"Well, you see that man next to my dad? You know anything about him?"

Dr. Cohen looks at the photograph again, this time not quite as closely. "Sure do. Name's Michael. He was a godsend to us kids, I can tell you that. Made us feel as if we were special. Not 'special' as in being outcasts who weren't like normal, healthy kids, special as in we were individuals with a problem in our lives, but we were not the problem ourselves. Know what I mean?"

"Yeah, I guess so. Do you know what became of him? Where he went? Where he is now? My dad said you two had an even more special bond than all the rest of the kids."

He laughs a short laugh. "Ah, I don't know about all that. I do know he affected me in a pretty profound way. Doesn't take a professional shrink to see how he influenced me to do what I do."

Angie blushes lightly, recalling the conversation with her father the night before. Dr. Cohen gives no indication he has noticed. "Do you know where he is, though?" she presses.

"No, I'm afraid I don't, although he'd have to be collecting Social Security by now, I'd imagine. The last time I saw him was a cold January morning, at the funeral of my grandfather." He gives her back the photograph, placing it in her palm between her index finger and thumb. With a triggered reflex, like a lobster claw snapping, her fingers close on the picture.

Angie looks at him, summoning the nerve. "Dr. Cohen, you mind if I ask how he died?"

"Michael? I have no idea." He looks at her as if she just asked him why the moon was made of green cheese.

"Your grandfather."

"My grandfather? Well, I'm not sure where you are going with this, but I'll play along. The short answer is he died of exposure, but actually, he died of brain cancer. He was really sick and was about to die and…I don't know, maybe it was the breaking apart of his synapses or something. He got it in his head that it would be a good time to go sledding." He pauses, mentally transported back through the years. Angie is stunned, her mouth open. She snaps it shut, trying to stay in the moment, remain a pro. *When the going gets tough, the tough gets weirded out*, she thinks, then poises for the setup.

"Dr. Cohen, this Michael guy, I believe he was in the vicinity of two other deaths—maybe murders—recently." She rushes onward, sensing he's about to interrupt. "Two elderly people, from different states, both terminally ill, died recently while sledding. Sledding! And they were known to be acquaintances of a black male nurse who looks exactly like the man in this photograph." She taps the photo for emphasis.

Dr. Cohen looks at her incredulously. Then he puts his head back and laughs. "Oh, my goodness. *That*, young lady, is a really good case for a mystery, but I just can't follow the chain of evidence linking the man I knew at summer camp to his finding the Fountain of Youth by playing Dr. Kevorkian in a docudrama about the Grateful Dead." He laughs again at his joke.

As he stops laughing, Dr. Cohen straightens out his lab coat. Angie just looks at him, not having gotten the reaction she was expecting. "Angie, I'm going to step into the boys' room here for a minute. Would you be so kind as to wait for me in the Tomorrow's Fund Clinic waiting room upstairs?" Without waiting for an answer, he ducks into the bathroom, steps to the sink while loosening his bow tie, and bends over the sink. Running the cold water, he cups his hands together and scoops water onto his face. Looking up, he blinks several times, lets out a long, slow breath, and dries his face and hands. He takes in a few more deep breaths, reties his tie, smooths back his hair, and tries to compose himself.

All right, he thinks, looking at himself in the mirror. *It's been a long time, and it's a long road back. Haven't thought about that summer or that fateful January snowy night…wow, it seems like since forever. Michael. Grandpa John. When he died, it broke my heart. I loved him so much. I cried and cried. That was one of the saddest times of my life, on top of being sick. Then I began to get better, almost day by day. Like Grandpa was coming into me and driving the cancer cells out. I know it doesn't work that way, but, heck, I'm…*He studies himself in the mirror, making sure his eyes are clear. He winks at his reflection. *Now go out there and give that girl what she's really here for, whether she knows it or not.*

CHAPTER 13

Feats

As Angie steps off the elevator, she can see the colorful TOMORROW FUND sign, each letter a different, bright color, and she sees the entrance to the clinic is across the way. It is located in the left corner of an octagonal walkway. The center area is completely wide open, looking down to the atrium below that features a tree, plants, and bright lighting from the skylights above. On the right wall, adjacent to the entrance of the clinic, is the children's hospital's own version of a zoo, with built-in glass chambers cut into various shapes. The resident and natural habitats include the North

American spotted turtle, the Australian snake-necked turtle, and the Rose Hair Tarantula. Also on the right wall are colorful hand molds of children, with their names etched underneath.

Preoccupied, Angie drifts to her recent encounter with the doctor. *The way Dr. Cohen's grandfather died—on a sled—makes three, and I can tie Michael directly to two of them. Maybe he has a really good plastic surgeon, Botox, and some great hair color helper. Whatever. If I can tie Charlie Fife to it, too, I have a story.* She crosses her legs and begins to jiggle her foot. *The text thing, though—that, I don't like. Not too comfy with that part. Don't get freaked. You're in public.* She can't help but look around to see if anyone's watching her. No one is. *Maybe I should call Dad and have him come get me. Or Jack.* She imagines the damsel-in-distress phone call to him: *"Oh Jaa-aack! Yoo-hoo! I'm looking for a white knii-iight!"* She stops the fantasy short before it can fully flower. *It'd help if he had a car, though, more than a stallion. Hey, Angie, get over it. You can always outrun...whomever.*

A short time later, the clinic door slowly opens and in walks Dr. Cohen, in conversation with what looks like someone from the hospital's staff. She is an attractive, forty-year-old, stylishly dressed woman carrying a Starbucks coffee. The tone of their conversation is light and they are smiling. Dr. Cohen stops just inside the entrance, and while he is still listening to his companion, he looks around as if looking for something or someone. He spots Angie, and with his arm, guides the woman he is with in Angie's direction. Angie returns the smile and stands to greet them.

"Good morning again, Angie," says Dr. Cohen.

Angie reaches and shakes Dr. Cohen's hand, and the hand of his companion.

"Angie Clarke, this is Katie Sosa, our parent consultant at the Tomorrow Fund. Katie, this is Angie Clarke, a new friend of mine and a daughter of an old friend of mine. She's here to do a story, I think. So perhaps you could provide her some background on what we all do here?" Both Angie and Katie exchange pleasantries.

"I don't mean to rush off, and Angie, I'll return in a bit. I have something I need to attend to, and would like to spend some extra time with you, so let me adjust my calendar. Would it be okay if I ask Katie to spend some time with you?"

"Well, sure, of course," she says. "But I don't want to be a bother and take everyone's time. In fact, my real questions were concerning Michael. Really, I could come back, if it's a problem." Dr. Cohen reaches with both hands and cups Angie's hands in his.

"No, it's no bother, and I would like to catch up with you. Just give me a few minutes. And yes, we'll discuss Michael, but getting exposed to some of this background information about what we do here couldn't hurt, okay?"

Dr. Cohen places his right hand on Katie's left shoulder, and after a gentle pat, he turns away and walks down the corridor, disappearing around the bend. Katie guides Angie into a side office, adjacent to what looks like a play area for children undergoing treatment, or waiting to be seen by the medical staff.

"Have a seat, Angie," says Katie, getting up and indicating a chair across the table from her. "Dr. Cohen does this sort of thing a lot. He 'facilitates.' He might pretend he's doing so without design or specific purpose, but those of us who've been around him for a while know he is a very purpose-driven man. He's one of my favorite people."

They both sit, a plush pile carpet muffling the sound of their chairs. Katie readjusts her shoulder-length black hair, so its two parted halves get tucked behind her ears. She sits forward, placing both hands on the table, facedown.

"Are you from around here?" asks Angie.

"Yeah, not too far. I was born in New Bedford, my dad is first generation from Portugal. After getting married, I settled in East Providence, just down Route 195 a little way. How about you?"

"Oh, I'm from Arlington, Mass, and go to school at Syracuse. So my dad and Dr. Cohen were childhood friends, and I'm doing a story on something, and wanted to meet Dr. Cohen and get his thoughts."

"He's a wonderful man, and loved by so many. I don't think I've ever met any doctor who has such a caring heart. He took care of my son, Adam."

"Your son was sick? How's he doing?" asks Angie in a chipper tone.

Katie politely smiles, knowing all too well the awkwardness that's about to settle into the room.

"He passed away five years ago," Katie says softly. "He would have been thirteen this coming Christmas Eve."

"I'm so sorry," says Angie, her eyes lowering toward the tabletop.

"It's OK. Thank you, though," says Katie like a seasoned professional. "Adam was very brave, a real little warrior through the whole thing. He went through so much. He had osteosarcoma, a bone cancer. He had chemo, surgery, radiation—you name it, he had it. He was a lot braver than we were, that is for sure. My husband and I went through a lot. Cancer—any disease, actually—is an extremely difficult thing to watch your child go through. You would do anything to save your child and stop the disease from spreading and stop the suffering. You'd trade places with your child in a heartbeat." She pauses again, her eyes unflinchingly holding Angie's. She clears her throat, the only external indication of her internal emotions. "But it doesn't work that way."

"No, I know," says Angie. "I almost hate to ask this, but how do you get back from something like that. How do you recover?"

"Well, part of you doesn't. You leave that part with your child, and you visit it when you are about to go to sleep, maybe, or when you see something that reminds you of your child. You keep that part separate from your everyday life. I have two other children and I can't cheat them of my attention because I lost a son. They lost a brother. And my husband—Adam was his little man. You give each other space to grieve and you don't avoid talking about him, but you can't let the grief take over or it will destroy you—and everyone else. The trick is knowing when to share your feelings so no one drifts too far away in their pain, and when to process your feelings in your own mind so that you can maintain your everyday lives. That's the difficult part." She stops and considers what she just said. "Let me rephrase that—that is *one* of the difficult parts."

Angie, amazed at Katie's forthright honesty, can't find a question she thinks worthy of the moment. Katie looks down, shuffles through some papers in a manila folder, takes out a pen, and makes a notation on the cover of a magazine. She closes the folder and pushes it toward Angie. "Take this home with you. There are some materials in there for you to read later," she says.

Looking back up at Angie, Katie continues, "Now, to answer your question, let me tell you what I did to help 'recover,' as you put it. What I did was come back. I got very used to the people here, the doctors, the nurses, the orderlies, the technicians—everybody. They had become like family, we were all in this really intense fight together, and everyone, all of them strangers until the day we first brought Adam in here, was just so wonderful, kind and loving. How could I not come back?"

"Wasn't it painful?" Angie asks. "Coming back to where…you know, your son died?"

"For some people," says Katie, "it *is* painful to revisit the physical location where they lost a child. For me, it was healing. The only way I could take stock of what happened, and to allow some healing to take place, was to be around others who either had been through, or were going through, such an enormously profound experience as what I had gone through. And by meeting with and talking to other parents whose children were traversing the ups and downs of cancer treatment, I found some degree of comfort, some understanding of what had happened to my son, and, just as importantly, what had happened to my family, and to me. Then I could heal, and I could help my whole family heal. As much as possible, that is. After three years here, I don't think they could keep me away unless they changed the locks."

"So do you work here every day?" asks Angie.

"Just about," says Katie. "They always seem to leave a little something for me to do to make me feel useful. Besides, there is always some family that could use a hand organizing all of the…things that go into having a child come through these doors. Sometimes a parent just needs somebody to talk to, someone to cry with them, someone who's been where they are. There are two of us called parent consultants, which is probably a polite, shortened term for the been-there-done-that people." She laughs at her wry joke.

"That's amazing, Katie. I can't imagine being as brave as you," says Angie, blushing as soon as the words are out of her mouth.

Katie laughs, deflecting praise. "Oh, you give me too much credit, Angie. Coming here helps me more than I help them." She stops laughing and stands up. "C'mon, let's take a walk around and see the clinic. I'll show you what bravery looks like."

Angie gets up, too, and the two women begin to walk through the family area. Katie begins to give her some background, the seemingly rehearsed, less personally revealing, prepared part of her tour.

"In the state of Rhode Island," she begins, "we are the only local nonprofit organization that provides financial and emotional support to children with cancer who are treated at

Hasbro hospital, and to their families. Dr. Cohen has always said that when a child is diagnosed with cancer, we obviously need to treat the child, but we also treat and support his or her family."

"How many children have cancer?" Angie asks, as they walk past a waiting room where a girl, perhaps four years old, is playing with an Elmo doll on an immaculate blue carpet, while her parents watch, both nervous with hands twisted together in their laps.

"Good question, Angie. Estimates are that in the United States alone, about twelve thousand five hundred children are diagnosed each year with some form of cancer. But consider this—UNICEF estimates six hundred million people are born with or acquire a disability in their lifetime. Of those, twenty-five percent, or a hundred fifty million, are children. And hundred and fifty million are kids. Every time I say it, I can't get my head around that number."

Angie and Katie walk by a playroom, where several young girls are coloring. A volunteer is cutting pieces of construction paper for them. Another woman, sitting with a girl hooked up to an IV, looks up. "Hi, Katie," the woman says. "Love your outfit."

"Thanks, Nicole," answers Katie. "As the French say, Targét." She gets down to eye level with the woman's daughter, and asks, "How's Olivia doing this morning?"

"Good," the little girl answers, voice pleasant, but thin.

"That's good," says Katie to her. "You hang in there, okay?"

"I will," she answers. Her smile, real, innocent, and directly from the heart, emerges from under the caves formed by dark circles beneath her sunken eyes. The contrast, sun from out of the darkness, is striking.

They walk on and Katie turns to Angie, and once they are out of earshot of the mother and child, Katie says, "Now do you see why I can't stay away? To be around courage like that, I mean, that little girl is being bombarded by Adriamycin right now, and that's why she looks flushed underneath her paleness. It's hot and the next time she has to pee, it's going to be red. That's from the chemo, but she doesn't understand that. She'll think it's her blood. And even though she'll have seen it before, she'll be terrified. But did you hear her complain?"

"No, I never would have known, Katie," Angie says.

"But her mother, Nicole, she didn't complain either," Katie adds. "In fact, she made a point of complimenting me on my dress. That is the definition of strength, right there. Pretending everything is normal when it most definitely is not. She does that for her child, even though everything in her is probably making her want to break down and scream for someone, or something, to make everything better so she doesn't have to watch her child hurt anymore. She'll break later. That's when she'll need me to help *her*."

They continue through the area, and walking through a door reading Medical Staff Only, a back entrance to the "inner sanctum," as Katie refers to it, they see Dr. Cohen sitting on the floor, a child standing facing him, with the doctor's stethoscope earpieces in his ears and the business end of the instrument pressed to the doctor's chest. They both turn toward Angie and Katie. The boy, maybe five years old, has an eye patch over his left eye, white and blue-striped polo shirt, and a bandana wrapped around his head. And like the majority of the children Angie has seen today, he has no hair.

"Hi, gang! Care to join us?" Dr. Cohen says, sounding more like a kid on a playground than the chief oncologist and medical professor.

"Well, I certainly could use a checkup," Katie says, advancing toward the two. "Why don't you let me sit over there by the window and you can count my heartbeats, okay, Teddy?" She and the boy go over near a wall covered with colorful cutouts of animals, while Dr. Cohen gets up from the floor and joins Angie.

"Have a good talk with Katie, Angie?" he asks, smiling pleasantly.

"Yes, she is really something," Angie answers. "To go through what she has and still want to help others, it's…inspiring."

"I'm glad you're inspired," he says. "That's a good thing. Now, do you have any questions for me, or shall I just lecture like I do at fundraisers and conferences?"

"Well, I noticed the way you got down to the boy with the pirate outfit and let him take your heartbeat. Is that one of the ways you build trust?"

"Yes, that's one of the ways to reassure the child that what you are doing to him is safe, but—and I don't mean to make you feel badly, Angie—but Teddy isn't really 'playing' pirate. He has something that's called retinoblastoma, cancer of the eye. We had to remove his left eye."

"Oh, God, Dr. Cohen, I feel like such a jerk. I had no idea."

"Angie, you had no way of knowing, and that's the point," Dr. Cohen says kindly. "Most people see a kid like Teddy there, and if they don't think he's playing Captain Bligh, they think something happened, like he had it poked out or whatever. The point is, he's a kid and that's all he wants to be. He doesn't want to be felt sorry for, he doesn't want you to treat him any differently, like someone who needs to be coddled or babied. He just wants to be what he is—a bright child who loves to play, watch Power Rangers, and learn to read. Yes, even with one eye."

"Yeah," says Angie "I get it. I'd feel the same way, I guess. I just never thought about it that way, although I had a friend who was really sick once, and I played with her every day. Until she died, that is." *I wish I'd left that part out*, she thinks, feeling herself redden.

Dr. Cohen notices her full blush of embarrassment and attempts to assuage her feelings. "It's okay, Angie," he says softly. "Unfortunately, some children *do* die, although we try not to stress that too much here until it becomes…necessary. Enough of the Grim Reaper talk. I've got more to show you."

Walking along, he points out the different pod areas where children from about five to ten years of age are all sitting, playing or dozing as they undergo their chemo treatments, or, in some cases, are waiting to get wheeled into the rooms where they'll undergo radiation. Infusion tubes are the norm here, and no one seems to give them a second glance when a new patient is brought into the room with tubes attached. There are a few adolescents sprinkled in amongst the younger patients. Several PlayStations buzz, whir, and beep, and there are the sounds of children laughing and exclaiming disgust when they lose a round. Everyday sounds that leaven the seriousness of their circumstances.

"Surprised by all this fun activity? In a hospital, no less?" asks Dr. Cohen. Angie doesn't take her eyes off the children.

Dr. Cohen takes a few steps out from behind Angie, and is besieged with cheerful hellos from the children, parents, and staff. "This is my favorite and most special place in the world," he says. His face beams as he kneels down to receive a hug from a little girl. He stands up and motions to the nurses at the nurses' station that he would return in a minute. He then turns to Angie and motions with his hand for her to follow him.

"This way, Angie," says Dr. Cohen. Angie is in a sort of trance, as she can't take her eyes off the children. Dr. Cohen waves to those calling his name. "Can you imagine how privileged I feel coming here and being inspired by these children every day? I'm so fortunate to have them in my life, you know?" says Dr. Cohen. "They thank me for stuff all the time, and I appreciate it, but I'm the most thankful man in the room. Each and every child is an inspiring story. They teach me something new about living every day."

"With all due respect, Doctor, you are a very special man," says Angie. "Doesn't it ever get overwhelming?"

They are talking near a wall, covered from floor to ceiling with the hand molds of children, each with a name underneath it. Dr. Cohen reaches out to trail his fingers lightly over several of them before answering.

"No, Angie, I find this work invigorating. It makes me a better parent, and a better person for getting to know them. These children are faced with life-threatening illnesses, just like I was. Just like your father was. And their families—brother, sisters, parents, grandparents—they all come in here to support them. These people here display the best of the human spirit. They are all my heroes. You know how society puts celebrities on a pedestal and everyone thinks pro football or baseball players are great athletes? Well, they are, granted, very specialized, trained performers who choose to do what they do with their bodies. *Performers.* But some of the kids here? They aren't performing; they're *surviving.* And they didn't choose to put their bodies through the hell they go through. Their athleticism is built around *surviving.* When the degree of difficulty is thrown into the mix? The incredibly powerful and often toxic drugs, the killing off of cells—the good ones as well as the very bad ones—inside their brains and bodies. The surgeries, the removal of organs, the amputations." He stops and looks at her. "Now, I'm going to introduce you to a real athlete."

They go to an examination room, and after knocking on the door and waiting for a response, they enter to see a boy about twelve years old in a wheelchair, with his father, a tall man, especially when juxtaposed next to his son. Slightly hunched over in his wheelchair, the boy apparently has some trouble coordinating his eye and head movements. But his eyes, which are reddened, find Dr. Cohen's, and he breaks into a wide grin.

"Hey, Zac! How's it going today? They treatin' you okay here at the Bloodtest Hotel?"

The boy laughs. "Good one, Doc. Bloodtest Hotel. Yeah, they just never put any back, know what I'm sayin'? It's all take, take, take around here!"

"Well, you know, blood like yours, it's pretty special, so we'll be careful with it. We'll make sure no vampires get it, you can bank on that."

"As in blood bank, Doc?" Zac is beaming now.

"Good comeback, Zac," says Dr. Cohen. "Hey, this is Angie, she's doing a story on our little operation here, our blood bank, as you call it. Zac, Ron, meet Angie. Angie, meet Zac and Ron." After allowing them all to exchange hellos, Dr. Cohen reaches out to tousle Zac's hair. "Well, we'll leave you in the good hands of the nurses here. Maybe see you at the pool next week?"

"Sure, Doc. I'll be there," Zac says. His speech is slightly slurred.

After they close the door and walk on down the hall a dozen feet, Dr. Cohen turns to Angie. "Zac has a disease called ataxia-telangiectasia, or A-T, for short. It's neurodegenerative and affects all of his muscular movements. While he may have a slower response time to some visual clues, he, as you can see from meeting him, is perfectly normal in terms of grasping the nuances of speech, and other than the muscular restrictions, can function in everyday life just as any twelve-year-old.

"And the muscular problems are severe. But—and this is where the athleticism I was telling you about comes into play—you put him in a pool and you should see the transformation. With a water noodle under his arms, he'll take a basketball and motor around the pool as if he was LeBron James going in for a slam dunk. The only difference is perspective. From my point of view, Zac there has more significant hurdles to get over to play water basketball than a pro basketball player does on a hardwood floor on healthy legs. Zac's tough as nails and doesn't know the meaning of the word 'quit.' With a little luck, along with his drive to thrive, not just survive, Zac will have a good, long life."

"Is A-T like cancer, then?" Angie asks.

"No, it's not. But as if the A-T wasn't enough, people with A-T have a much higher likelihood of developing cancer than so-called normal people do," he answers. "During some routine tests, we found some swelling in his lymph glands, and so we have to follow up with more tests. We'll keep our fingers crossed."

"I'll say some prayers for him, Dr. Cohen," says Angie.

He looks at her. "Prayers are good, Angie. As they say, 'Pray to God but row toward shore.' What we do here is the rowing part. Lots and lots of rowing toward shore."

Angie considers the statement, and is about to say something, but Dr. Cohen starts talking before she begins. "Now,

Angie, I have to get on with the rest of my rounds, and you can't come into some of the places I have to visit, and I know you came here to ask some questions about a man I knew a long time ago. I don't know how I can help you with that, other than to tell you, as a medical professional and a man of science, that humans are all prone to the natural laws of aging and mortality, and you are asking about a man. Now, as a man who believes in a power greater than ourselves, I can tell you I wish you luck in your search for…whatever it is you are looking for."

"Uh, Dr. Cohen? I…" Angie starts, hoping her mind will catch up to her open mouth with formulated words to keep Dr. Cohen from leaving. She fails.

"You have the folder Katie gave you? When you get home, or later, look it over. There's an article on page thirty-three in the *Children's Health* magazine in there that you might find interesting. Now, it was great meeting you, and give my best to Cliff." He shakes her hand, smiling as he does so, and quickly turns and walks away, nodding to a nurse, who joins him as they head down the hall.

"What? Wait!" Angie yells to him across the foyer, but he continues to walk away.

CHAPTER 14

Transon Be Told

T he trip back to Arlington starts inauspiciously when Angie has trouble finding her car. Remembering the text when she arrived, and recalling her recent discovery that another elderly person, Dr. Cohen's grandfather, died while the mysterious Michael was at least in the vicinity, she is feeling more than a little unnerved. Unraveling by the second, she finds a security guard and tells him she thinks the car might have been stolen. He tells her that a lot of people forget where their car is because of the ordeal they've just gone through in the hospital. Driving her up and down the rows of parked cars, they find it, and he watches to make sure she gets in okay. She's relieved to have had the company.

It's been some day, she thinks as she heads up I-95. *Confirmation of another homicide or murder, a meeting with some incredible people, and a visitation from a spirit friend I used to play dolls with. Oh, yeah, and texts from a stalker. I wish I hadn't been so pigheaded and kept that to myself. Oh, well, I never would have gotten here otherwise. Somebody would have stopped me. Just drive the speed limit and don't let anyone weird-looking box you in.*

Turning into her driveway, she stops and thinks about what she will and won't tell her parents when they get home in a few hours. She gets her handbag, notices the folder sticking up out of it, and is about to take it out when her phone, set to ring again, goes off. With a feeling of dread and foreboding, she takes it out and unlocks the screen, sees she has a text, opens it. "GKTW." She turns it off, tosses it in her bag, and pivots her neck left, then right, making sure there's no one on either side of her or behind her.

She's out of her car and up the three steps, and, smooth and efficient with her key, inside within fifteen seconds, door slammed and locked behind her. She takes stock of the situation. She opens the curtain in the living room and peeks outside, seeing no one outside or lurking in a car nearby. She walks into the dining room and looks out a window there. No one. Does the same drill out the kitchen window. Nobody there, either. Satisfied, she sits down at the kitchen table, reflecting on her situation as the weak midafternoon sun slants through the window, casting the decorative bottles on the windowsill as silhouetted shadows on the wall to her right. Twirling her hair, she settles down, realizes she's hungry, gets a bag of Oreos and a glass of milk, and sits back down at the table with them. The perfect midafternoon meal for someone feeling confused, overwhelmed, and yes, Angie would admit, a little frightened.

I should do something, she muses. *I'm on a roll.* She gets her phone from her bag, grabs the phone book from its spot on the small side table next to the kitchen table. She finds the name Fife and dials, part of her hoping there will be no answer and she can have a reprieve from the increasingly confusing and complex story she's taken on. No such luck. A female's voice picks up on the third ring.

"Hello!" More of a declaration than a question.

"Hello, my name is Angela Clarke, and I'm looking for a Mrs. Vera Fife."

"Well, hi there, Angela Clarke, this is Vera. I've been expecting your call."

You've been what? thinks Angie before following up. "Mrs. Fife, I am doing some work on a story for the *Arlington Advocate*, and I have some questions I'd like to ask you about your…late husband, Charlie. Is that okay? Is this a good time?"

"It's a perfectly good time, Miss Clarke, and I will call you Angie if you would be so kind as to call me Vera."

"Well, okay…Vera. I was wondering if you had information about a man your husband might have met the night he died?" *There, it's out there,* Angie thinks. *Heroes rush in where fools don't dare follow.* She's very proud of herself. For about a second.

"Angie, I said it was a perfect time. I didn't say it was a perfect *place.* The perfect place would be if you came over to our house. I promise I will answer all the questions I can. How does that sound?"

Remembering the texts and loathe to leave the safety of her childhood home, Angie has a moment of doubt. Knowing she can't afford to lose the opportunity to blow the story wide open, she goes ahead and says, "Sure, Mrs. Fife… Vera. I can be there in about…" She looks at the clock on the wall. "In about fifteen minutes. That okay?"

"See you then," says Vera. "You know where we live?"

Angie, catching the use of "we" instead of "I," attributes the pronoun usage to years of habit not easily undone. "I do, Vera. Walnut Terrace. I'll be there shortly."

Following a dash to the car after a thorough sequence of out-the-window peeking for potential stalkers, Angie is on the road and soon in front of the Fifes' house, a medium-sized, pale blue garrison, well kept, and already with Christmas lights strung along its outline. She surveys the outside of the home, noticing the breezeway and detached garage. *Oh, my God, this is just like my dream. Different colors but same layout and everything. Oh, my God! Keep calm, Angie Clarke. You can do this.*

She rings the bell, and the door opens before the echo of the first ding-dong has receded. A sturdy—but not too-much-so—woman in a dark blue dress with a black paisley pattern opens the door, and immediately breaks into a huge smile as she greets Angie. Her light blue eyes are the first—and for a moment, the only—thing Angie can take notice of. Caught by a shaft of light, the eyes show green flecks in the blue, and they seem capable of looking inside Angie's brain, capable of reading her thoughts, her intentions. Angie has to break off contact, embarrassed at what Vera might find there.

"Come on in, my dear friend, Angie Clarke! I've heard so much about you. What an honor and delight to finally meet you! Come in, come in. Let me take your coat."

Angie feels disoriented, taken off guard by the familiarity of the greeting. She goes in and takes a look around, then follows Vera past the stairway leading upstairs, through the dining room, and into the kitchen, where Vera walks to a door at one end and hangs Angie's jacket on a hook. *Oh, my God. That's where Old Charlie's coat was the night he...*

"Well, dear, taking a break from school, I understand? You know, Charles and I spent a few years in upstate New York right after we got married. In Troy. I still remember its motto—*Ilium fuit, Troja est*, which means, 'Ilium was, Troy is.' Well, one thing Troy *was* was cold. Don't miss those winters, I can tell you." They stand in the kitchen, Vera leaning with both arms on the back of a chair at the kitchen table, and Angie standing in the middle of the room, bag slung over her shoulder.

Angie, remembering the journalistic credo to establish rapport before jumping into the questions, tells Vera she's sorry about her husband's death. She's also a little surprised to find that she means it, more than just saying it because you're supposed to say it. "Everyone says what a wonderful man he was," she adds.

"Yes, Angie, he was a wonderful man. Married sixty years, we were. And thank you for your sympathies. It's an adjustment. It happened pretty suddenly, but I've got lots of friends and family to keep me busy and make sure I don't just sit there and feel sorry for myself. You know that old saying—'Everything happens for a reason,' don't you, Angie?"

"Yes, Vera, I do, but it still has to be tough to lose someone like your husband."

"Well, yes, but you also know how old sayings get to be old sayings, don't you?"

"I'm not sure I…" Angie starts.

Vera finishes. "Because they're true, my dear young Angie. Because they're true."

"I wish I was writing a story about him while he was still alive, rather than about his death," Angie says.

"Yes, his death. I know you want to talk about his death, and I know you have some questions about it, how it happened that night, and I promise I'll do my best to answer them—in a little while. You know, Charles was dying, Angie. He didn't make a big deal out of it, but he had pancreatic cancer and was afraid it had moved elsewhere. Metastasized, as they so wonderfully call such a thing. Death creeping about, is what it is. He was ready. We weren't all ready to see him go, of course, but Charles was ready to move on to the next adventure, as he called it. Anyway, there's something I'd like to show you, and someone I'd like for you to meet in a little bit. If you'd be so kind to come with me, please, I'll bring us in some banana bread and some tea in a bit."

Vera leads Angie back through the dining room and the formal living room to a room at the far, back end of the house. "Charles called this the den, although they're referred to as 'man caves' these days, I guess. Now, I think that's just an excuse for throwing bones they've eaten the flesh from, and the tools they used, on the floor when they're done with them." She laughs. The den, like the rest of the house, is not actually cavelike at all. Hardwood floors gleam, shown off by deep-pile Oriental rugs and tasteful colonial-style antiques.

Pointing to a large, overstuffed leather chair with matching ottoman, Vera instructs Angie to sit there. A window just behind and to the left of the chair sends late afternoon sunlight onto its side, and the window muntins separating the panes cast barred shadows in perfect geometry.

"Oh, no, I'll be fine right here," says Angie, moving to sit in a stiff, ladder-backed chair with slab rattan caning.

"No!" blurts Vera. She surprises Angie, and herself, with the force of her directive, and she quickly tries to soften it down. "I mean, really, dear, please sit in *that* one. Charles loved to sit there."

Angie, still taken aback by Vera's tone, backs into the chair, watching Vera warily. *Whoa,* she thinks, *looks like Vera here is getting in touch with her inner kindergarten teacher. Hope she doesn't go all Cruella De Vil on me. Why can't I just have a normal interview in which I get to ask my questions before the dog and pony show?*

"There," Vera says as Angie gets settled in the large chair. The seat envelopes her, broken in by many years as a host to people's posteriors. It makes a small squishing sound as she adjusts her rear end to get comfortable. The puckered leather feels substantial through her thin pants, almost regal, as if befitting a throne.

"Put your feet up!" chirps Vera. She watches as Angie complies, a wide grin playing across her face, an elderly version of the Cheshire Cat.

Angie, feeling more than a little awkward now, smiles weakly back at Vera, who remains standing just inside the den's doorway, hands clasped together at her chest, still smiling radiantly. Angie moves to get her notebook from her bag as she unhooks it from her shoulder.

"No, no, no! Just put that aside for now, Angie. You need to just relax! Feel. Relax and *feel*."

Angie is about to ask Vera how she can relax with someone practically yelling at her to relax as she moves the notebook to lay her handbag at the side of her chair. It slips out of her grasp and tips over on its side. The folder with the magazine Katie gave her at the hospital slides partway out of the bag. She looks at it lying on the floor for a second. Angie notices Vera has tracked what she's looking at and is now looking at it as well.

Vera breaks off the moment, which feels like a stalemate of sorts to Angie. "We'll get to everything in good time, Angie. I didn't mean to sound harsh, but we're just so excited to have you here. Now, you stay here while I go fix us something to eat. And my grandson, Chas, is here, too. He has so been looking forward to meeting you; he should be down shortly. Be back in a jiff!"

Did she really say "jiff"? Angie asks herself. *I hope she means she'll be back soon, not that she'll be back in a jar of peanut butter.* She grins to herself, pleased with her wit. She feels herself actually do what Vera ordered and relax. Giving a passing thought to getting up and walking around the room, she discovers she really doesn't want to. She studies the room from her perch in the chair and glances over to the mantel above the fireplace. There is a row of photographs, the usual sort of family fare: kids huddled together in their good clothes in front of Christmas trees, a beaming boy in front of a birthday cake decorated with lit candles, and a boy in a wheelchair next to a fishing boat. The boy in this last photo appears to be an older version of the boy in front of the birthday cake, but it's difficult to be certain from across the room. There is an older man she's sure is Old Charlie Fife on one side of the boy in the chair. But there is another man flanking the wheelchair on other side. He's half-shadowed by something on the dock just outside the photograph, but she can see his left arm, and the left side of his neck and face is dark. He's wearing a hat as well, making his features harder to distinguish but she's sure she knows who it is. She'd like to ponder this thought a little more, knows it's important, but can't quite focus on *why* it's important, and how to place this knowledge into any contextual framework that will instruct her as to what she should do with this knowledge.

I can't believe how tired I am, she thinks. *Couldn't have been drugged. Never had the Jif. Ha! Well, it's been a long day. It's warm in here. Closing my eyes can't hurt. I'm sure Miss Bossy Pants will wake me up.* She closes her eyes. She opens them, not willing to give in to sleep, finds she can't keep her eyes open, and closes them again. Feels herself drift, not asleep but drifting... and then *boom!* She's yanked outside of herself, but still there, still present, maybe more present in a moment than she's ever felt before. *Feels cold air, like a hard, fast body slam from a forechecking forward on the hockey pond. Her face feels the rush of cold, moist air, and her body, pressed chest down on something flat, is flung weightless into space. She feels ground underneath her now, bouncing, falling, bumping along the ground, and hurtling downward. She's exhilarated, overcome with emotion, transformed. "Wow! I haven't been sledding in years," she feels her inner self say, even as she is aware of another self—a cocooning outer self—overriding her conscious thought. She feels herself picking up speed, as if that was possible, a brief slowing down of her dream vehicle, and then whoosh! She's airborne, free of Earth's binding restrictions, floating. Then a cushioned landing and it's off downhill again, chilled damp air rising from the snow to make her skin tingle. Then, steered by an unseen hand—she's pretty sure, anyway, that it's not her—she sweeps to a snowplowing stop, burying her face in wet, loose, unpacked snow.*

Angie shakes her head briskly from side to side, as if shaking snow off her face. Opening her eyes as she does so, she wipes her hand across her face, fully expecting to find it wet. It isn't. She shakes her head again, a smaller gesture this time, more to clear her head. She looks around the room and sees she has company. Vera is sitting on a small loveseat, knees held primly together, and her hands lie folded in her lap. Seated in the ladder-backed chair is a brown-haired boy, about ten, with black rectangular glasses, smiling broadly at her. He looks at her expectantly, as if he can't wait to hear what she has to say. The specific feelings from her recent chair ride fall away, but their warmth remains. She notices the boy has a pair of metal crutches and silver-colored titanium leg braces, with perpendicular straps attached to them, leaning against the right arm of his chair.

"Yes, *and*...what happened?" the boy blurts.

"Chas, where are your manners?" asks Vera gently. "Let the young woman get her bearings, let her get her feet back on the ground, as it were." She pauses and turns to Angie.

"Angie, this is Chas, our grandson. Chas, this is Angie, whom you've heard so much about. Well, Angie, like Chas said, what happened? You have a nice ride?"

Angie, feeling like someone taken from a nap and dropped onstage in a foreign country, slowly looks from Chas to Vera, then back again. "What just happened? And how did you... how do you...know..." She trails off.

"Angie, I think you just went sledding," Vera says calmly. Chas nods, still grinning ear to ear.

"But…how?" Angie bounces her glance back and forth between the two again, as if watching two skilled tennis players volleying.

"Well, Angie, the physics are a little vague, if that's what you're asking," says Vera. "But it happens. It happens. In that chair it does, anyway. I don't know how he does it, or who's helping him do it. Those are most likely unanswerable—at least on this earth—but I do know that it's my Charles doing the steering. I also know not everyone gets the ride. In fact, other than Chas here, the only one who does—has—is you, dear."

"But why? And why me? I mean, did you know…that I'd get the ride, as you call it?"

"Wasn't sure. But we have had…um, *indications*, you might say, that you were a person of interest in these matters. Gosh, that sounds so formal, but it will have to do for now. Now, there's something else we'd like you to see. Chas?"

Angie starts to say something in response to Vera's ambiguity, but is caught tongue-tied as Chas abruptly grabs a hold of his crutches, like one familiar with reaching for them as a matter of course, a hockey player grabbing his stick before taking his shift on the ice. "Hey, Angie," he says. "How about we trade places?"

As she gets up, still at a loss for words, Chas attaches his crutches, carefully strapping himself in, even though it's only about ten steps from his side of the room to hers. Angie notices how frail and unsubstantial the boy's body is. Strapped in, Chas crosses over and the two make an awkward couple as they switch places, and he almost falls as a crutch gets caught in the strap of her handbag.

"Oh, my God, I am so sorry!" she says, mortified.

"No, Angie, I wasn't watching where I was walking," he says. "Walking, get it? With a crutch? Walking?"

Angie smiles, not knowing if it's okay to do so.

"Funny boy, Chas, funny boy," Vera chimes in, letting Angie know it's an old, tried-and-true routine. Making light to remove the sting.

Chas settles himself down into the chair, using the armrests to slow his descent. He lifts his legs with his hands underneath his knees, and sets them on the otto-man. Angie sits straight-backed in the chair he just vacated. With a quick glance at Vera, who's watching Chas intently, Angie gets as comfortable as she can in the archaic piece of furniture. *No wonder the Puritans were so darn unhappy all the time*, she thinks. She turns her attention back to Chas.

Eyes closed, small, private smile on his face. He sits perfectly still for a moment and then he begins to grin. Then, like sunlight emerging from behind a storm cloud, his face turns radiant, a child's face emitting light, as pure a sight as

Angie has seen. She gets ambushed by the purity of emotion and feels herself about to cry.

Angie knows where he is, having just returned from a similar experience. *But there's more to this feeling*, she thinks. *Imagine the difference between not being able to walk freely and then taking that ride. I only had the difference between knowing what it's like to walk and riding free on that celestial sled. The degree of freedom for him has got to be amazing. I feel so incredibly good for him.* Angie feels a dam break inside her, and tears begin to stroll down her cheek, uncontested by self-restraint. Chas gives no indication he's hearing, and Vera just looks over at her and smiles. "Let it go, girl, it's okay. Let it go." The woman knows when to let people be.

The three stay in the moment, three spiritual beings stuck in amber, unconcerned with the passage of time. Soon, all three come back to the present. Chas speaks first.

"Boy! I just can't get over what it's like. Hey, Angie, Grandpa stick you in the snow, too?"

"Yes, Chas, he did. Playful guy, isn't he?" She is still struggling with the idea that a dead man can steer any sled, much less someone else's sled, but she feels she owes it to the people in this room and the sanctity of the moment to at least consider believing in the idea.

"Sure is!" Chas says.

Angie looks over at Vera, who is already holding out a handkerchief, arm extended to Angie. "Vera, I have never seen anything like this! I mean, I haven't even read anything like this. What just happened is…incredible."

"Girl, you have not seen anything yet," says Vera. "Chas, show the girl. Young woman."

Chas looks over at Angie, and winks. "Okey-dokey," he says. He's got a self-possessed look on his face, half-smiling, but without the mirth of a couple of minutes ago. This is the look of someone who knows something—a profound truth—other people don't. "Here we go!"

With that, Chas takes his legs off the ottoman, sets them on floor, and stands up. No crutches, no braces. Takes a half turn from his spot between the chair and ottoman, and steps out and into the room, each foot lightly scraping the floor as he shuffles a little awkwardly out into the center of the room. He stops there. Beads of sweat break out on his forehead with the effort. His pants are wrinkled where the braces' straps grasp his knees. Then, after half a minute, he takes a few cautious steps toward Angie, pauses again, and then a few more, steadier now. He smiles fully at her now, no holding back his joy, and with mock solemnity, bows at the waist, one hand behind his back, the other extended, palm up, toward her. "I'd ask you to dance, but I'm a little rusty," he says. "Kind of like the Tin Man."

Angie stares at him, open-mouthed, and bursts into laughter, full-throated, unabashed laughter. Vera and Chas are right behind her, and they join in.

"This has got to be the most astounding day anyone has ever had, since, probably like *forever!*" is all she can say.

"Well said, Angie, well said," Vera tells her.

Chas backs up a couple of steps, keeping his eyes on Angie's, then moves side to side in a three-quarter crouch, like he's defending a point guard. He takes a slow pivot, almost slips, and then catches himself.

"Okay, fancy pants," says Vera. "You're not Fred Astaire. At least not yet, not until we figure out how all this works."

"I know, Grandma. Just seeing what I can do." Chas is obviously tiring, muscles slowly coming back to life, then fatigued back to quietude.

"Why don't we go back into the kitchen and have that snack I promised us?" Vera suggests on her way out of the room. "Chas, you want to gear up again?"

"I think so," he answers. He sits and puts his braces on, unassisted. Angie knows that to offer help would be patronizing. *He's fine*, she thinks. *Perfectly capable.*

Angie goes to pick up her handbag, puts the folder back inside. She turns around to leave, and passing by the mantel, takes a closer look at the photograph of the fishing expedition. She peers closely at it. The man's face is too obscured to be sure, but, like her dream—*hers and Old Charlie's dream, that is*—she adds to herself, it's the silhouette.

She looks back to Vera and then to Chas. Vera smiles and nods gently, signaling encouragement to Angie to go ahead and pick up the photograph. "Go ahead, dear. It's okay."

Angie focuses her eyes back on the frame and reaches out, picking it up for closer inspection. She slides her two fingers across the top, wiping away dust for a clearer view.

Chas's voice interrupts the silence. "Grandpa and I went to the Florida Keys. It was the best trip I've ever been on."

Angie slowly turns toward Vera. Angie's mouth is open in astonishment, pointing to one person in particular in the photograph. Vera nods as if reading her thoughts. "Yes, child," she says softly. The color in Angie's face drains and her knees begin to buckle, so she grabs the underside of the mantel with her right hand. Vera gets up from the couch, as best she can, to support Angie so she doesn't tumble, supporting her backside. "There, *there*, my dear."

"But it's…it's…it's…" Angie is aware of her stammering but can't quite steady her voice.

Still holding on to Angie, Vera says, "Yes, Angie. It is." Angie's hold on the photograph begins to loosen as her hands start to quiver. Vera takes a firmer grip and asks Chas to assist her. "Angie…Angie? My dear, are you okay?"

Angie relinquishes her grip on the photograph to Chas, just as she is about to drop it on the floor. She backs away, not blinking, almost in shock, and Vera helps her down to the ottoman. Angie motions to Chas that she would like to see the photograph again, and he obliges. Vera takes a seat next to Angie on the ottoman and Angie moves over to make some room. Vera points to the people in the picture.

"Let me tell you who these people are. You see, this is Chas, this is my husband and this is…"

Angie finishes Vera's sentence. "Michael. He hasn't changed at all," she says, awestruck. "So I'm right. There is something going on with him, isn't there? And you knew this all the time?"

They are all looking at a photograph that was taken recently. The boat in the picture is a sport fishing vessel. It is a thirty-six-foot twin engine white Bertram with a tuna tower. Both Chas and Old Charlie are standing in the aft section with large fishing poles at their side. On the transom of the boat is her name, the *Courageous Angel,* and standing behind the two, next to the captain of the fishing vessel, is Michael.

Angie pulls a section of hair from behind her head and begins to twirl. "I think I'm getting a headache," she says.

"You'll be okay, my dear," says Vera. "It's not every day you see an angel, a real-life one at that."

Angie slides back, as far as she can without falling off the ottoman. "An *angel*, you say? How can you be so sure? Maybe he's something quite the opposite, like a murderer or something."

Both Chas and Vera laugh out loud and Vera gets up from the ottoman. "Oh, no, my child, you have quite an imagination, don't you?"

"What do you say we have some banana bread and something to drink for that headache, and discuss this imagination of yours? Let's go into the kitchen and talk about it."

Vera and Chas beat Angie to the kitchen, are seated at the table, and there's a cup of tea steeping at an empty place along with a dish, and a whole loaf of banana bread in the center of the table, on a cutting board with a knife alongside it.

"So," starts Vera as Angie sits down, plopping her handbag next to the leg of her chair. "I would bet you have some questions, and I promised to answer them, so please feel free. Ask away!" She cuts off three Bible-thick hunks of bread, puts them on china plates, and passes one down the table to Angie.

Okay, thinks Angie, buying a little time by taking a big bite of bread and rinsing it down with a sip of tea. Something extraordinary just happened. I don't know what it was, but it did. *As Mr. Armstrong would say, "File it away and move forward." I still have questions. There's still a separate line of questioning. "Stay with what you know and stay on track. Record it, revisit it, reveal it. Then later, rewind it and reflect on it." That's what he'd say.*

She swallows, starts. "An angel, you say. Vera, I have been following a series of deaths, maybe murders, for a few weeks. Three grandparents have died, two recently and one a long time ago. What's a coincidence, and you know coincidences just don't just happen when murder's involved, is that all three died sledding, just like your husband." Turning toward Chas, she starts to apologize. "I'm sorry to bring your grandfather up like this but…"

"No apologies necessary, Angie," interrupts Vera. "Chas is perfectly aware of all of the conspiracy theories that have circulated about his grandfather. Go on." *That's odd*, Angie notes. *Vera is smiling.*

She continues. "So there's this one guy, a male nurse, who keeps showing up before the deaths. He's there at each one. Same guy every time. Now it's true, one of them happened probably forty years ago, but I'm still sure he's the same man who was there for all of them. Probably had plastic surgery or something. Like I said, coincidences don't just happen when it comes to people dying suddenly." *Maybe what I'm saying here will sink in if I keep saying it.*

"Angie, can I just say something here?" says Vera. "Not to take issue with your premise, but I do need to correct you on one thing *I* know to be true. Coincidences *do* happen. A coincidence is God's way of acting anonymously. Coincidences do happen, and not everything can be explained, nor can we expect everything to be explained by science, by footprint molds, or blood splatter patterns, or by imagined motivations by people we've never even met, in your case."

It's Angie's turn to interrupt. "Look, Mrs. Fife,"—going formal as if to punctuate the seriousness of her pronounce-ment—"the man who has shown up at each death is a man in a photograph you have on your mantel of Mr. Fife and Chas next to a fishing boat."

"Yes, I've gathered," says Vera.

Distracted, thrown off by Vera's casual response, Angie can only think to follow up with, "And that's it? You're not weirded out or anything?"

"The *Courageous Angel*. The name of the boat. The *Courageous Angel*." Vera is still seemingly unfazed by the conversation.

"Mrs. Fife—Vera—I think you're missing the point I am trying to make. The man in the photograph might be responsible for your husband's death." Still seeing no visible sign of distress on the elderly woman's face, or on Chas's, she decides to reveal her last and, she thinks, best card. "Mrs. Fife, I saw that man, the man by the side of the boat, in a dream I had. It was a dream about your husband, except I was kind of like…" She stalls, unsure of going all the way. "It was kind of like I was seeing the dream about him, but at the same time through him, if that makes any sense." *There, I said it*, she thinks.

"It doesn't matter if it makes any sense to me, Angie," says Vera. "Does it make sense to *you*? Does it have to?"

"I, uh, no, not totally, but…"

"Well, Angie, do you think everything in and about this whole universe we live in, the ground we walk on, and the air we breathe, and the water we drink, and the food we are given to eat can be explained in a scientific formula or equation?"

"No, I…well, yes *and* no, Vera," Angie says, looking to regain control of the interview. "I think there are a lot of things that don't have easy explanations. The Big Bang, things like that. The ride I just got in your husband's favorite chair. I don't know how something like that works, and Chas's being able to walk without braces after he took it. But I do believe we have to find answers to things. Like people dying. So I think the ride, and the dream I had, are your husband's way of telling me something. I think he knows who killed him, and those other people. I think he's trying to tell me, us, who did it."

"Well, you know, Angie, that's certainly one possibility. He could also just be telling us to stop our worrying about things and take a sleigh ride once in a while." Vera smiles. "Or—and this is what I believe to be true—he could be trying to give some strength and hope to people like Chas here. You saw how he walked afterward. Doesn't that mean something more than the death of a man who knew he was dying?"

"Arrgh! Vera, you keep answering a question with another question!" Angie closes her eyes, takes a breath, summons calm. "All right, I'll give you that I don't have explanations or anything for what happened in the chair. Or even in my dream. But this Michael guy—what do you know about him?"

"I know that was one of the most fun weekends I ever had when we all went fishing," says Chas. "We caught a lot of fish. We threw them all back after we 'tagged' them, and Michael let me ride on his back while he swam around the boat."

Angie looks at him, smiles weakly. "Okaaay," she says, drawing out the vowel. "But what do you know about him? Where did he come from? Where did he go? Where is he now? Where is he going next? Those are the important questions."

"I think he was heaven sent, I believe he went where he was needed, I believe that's where he is now, and I believe that's where he's going next. Those are the answers," says Vera. She looks now like the Cheshire Cat who has just swallowed a mouse.

This has Angie stumped. *How do I follow up with a second why with that answer?* "All right, I see where you're coming from, Vera." *Actually, I don't see where you're coming from at all,* she thinks. *But I do have one more card to play here.*

"There's one more thing. Ever since I started looking into this whole thing with the sleds and the old people—elderly people, sorry—and noticed that all of them had some child near and dear to them who was sick and needed a nurse nearby, I began to get text messages. Now, you can't be thinking your husband is sending me texts, too, can you? Tell me you don't believe that one."

Vera takes some time before answering. "What was in the text message? Anything specific? Anything you recognize?"

"No, Vera," says Angie firmly. "I don't know what it means. 'GKTW' is the only message whoever is writing it ever leaves."

"Can I see that magazine sticking out of your notebook?" Vera asks. Angie hands it to Vera, eyebrows raised and furrowed. Vera flips the pages while speaking. "I received the same magazine last week. I looked through it and saw something…hmm. Here it is." She stops turning pages and spins the magazine around so Angie can read it.

Angie reads the headline for the article: "Give Kids the World: Where Children Can Be Children." She leans in closer and reads the subhead underneath: "Seventy-acre nonprofit 'storybook' resort in Kissimmee, Florida, where children with life-threatening illnesses and their families are treated to a weeklong, fun-filled, cost-free vacation." Intrigued, she scans the page and sees there is a picture of a smiling boy in glasses that appear very large on his small head, sitting by an azure-colored swimming pool, surrounded by palm trees. He has a

T-shirt on with lettering across the front. The first letter of each word is in a capitalized cursive script, so that the letters GKTW stand out from the rest of the letters, announcing the location in which the boy is obviously sitting: Give Kids the World. Looking closer at the boy, she sees he is sitting in a wheelchair. And there, just over his left shoulder is Michael. He looks unchanged, just as she has seen him in the photo on the mantel, in her father's collection of photographs, and by the side of the Thompson girl at the funeral in Syracuse.

Startled yet again, she quells any outward sign of alarm this time, and in a deliberately level, steady voice, announces to Vera and Chas, "This is the guy I think is responsible for killing those old people—oops, sorry, Vera, I mean your husband and the other—"

"*Old* person," interrupts Vera, smiling broadly.

"Well, *elderly* person, then," amends Angie. "I know he was in the vicinity of those deaths. I saw him at the funeral of the woman in Syracuse. And now I think he's sending me those texts like some sort of stalker."

"Oh, my dear, I'm sorry you feel you're in some sort of peril, but I just don't see it that way."

"Are you kidding me? Is this some sort of joke, or a reality show where people ignore the obvious to make the one person in the world who can see things clearly feel as if she is blind?"

"No, it's no joke, my dear. I think it's evident that you just see danger where there is really safety. I believe Michael is a facilitator, an angel who has a very special mission, and it has nothing at all to do with death but has everything to do with life. With freedom for some very special people who have plenty of will themselves, but need some sort of additional inspiration, a boost, if you will. That's what I think is the catalyst contained in that chair," she says, nodding her head in the direction of the den.

Angie remembers a detail from her dream, something that'll perhaps make it just a dream. "Vera, did your husband have a cut on his hand the day he died?"

"Ha! That, he did. Bless my heart, he could be a clumsy oaf. Never was great with tools, although he tried. Yes, my Charles cut his hand, all right. Trying to wrangle the meat off the turkey. Lucky thing cranberry sauce can cover up some spilled blood. That way, he didn't have to make a big deal of it."

Angie nods, more to herself than to Vera and Chas. "Okay, Vera. I guess I'm out of questions, at least questions you can answer. I totally respect you and who you are. I still think there's something going on, and I am going to keep trying to find what it is. And as much as I believe what happened to me in that chair, and what happened to Chas in that chair, the whole thing feels like some weird episode of *The Twilight Zone*."

Vera laughs. "You're a very engaging and inquisitive young lady, Angie Clarke, and I really believe—I know, as a matter of fact—that you are going to go places. But I don't see any of this as *The Twilight Zone* at all, more like you visiting the home of Mickey Mouse. Florida, if you know what I mean." She stands up and goes around the table to hug Angie. "Don't forget your handbag!"

Angie says good-bye to Vera and Chas and heads for the door. She's just about at the door when Chas, still sitting at the table, calls out to her. She turns around to look at him. He grins at her, raises his extended right index finger and thumb to his right eye, snaps them quickly together like a camera shutter clicking, and winks.

CHAPTER 15

The Physics of It All

Darkness is taking back the day as Angie walks out to her car, the sky still smeared with a band of ruddy orange on the horizon to the west, even as houses are losing their sharpness of detail in the gloaming. Several stars are glittering to life and a blinking plane leaves a tiny white scratch, a contrail, in its wake. The streetlights are on, as are some lights over several of the doorways and garages in the neighborhood. *How could all this be so normal, while everything in my head is so not normal?* Angie thinks. *What a day. I'm so drained I could go to sleep here in my car. I need some real food. As in starch, sugar, carbs,*

steroids-fed beef, and goopy cheese all over a...sesame-seed bun! Good idea. Give myself time to think, not talk or listen. Fast food to slow down. Some place with Wi-Fi with my French fries.

Settled on a course of action, Angie takes the time to call her parents, and leaves a message saying she's going to grab some food and be home later. "Don't worry, Mom, Dad. Everything's fine," she tells the machine. "Just a little overwhelmed and hungry." She doesn't tell them she needs some time to sort through her day. *That'll just make them worry*, she thinks.

Angie heads south on Mass Ave., leaving Arlington. She takes a right onto Alewife Brook Parkway, heading into Cambridge, a little absentminded as she approaches the rotary where Alewife cuts through the busy crossing lanes that comprise the Concord Turnpike. Catching herself daydreaming about what she needs to figure out first before she goes home to write up her notes, she refocuses and slices through to the other side of the rotary. She remembers the old joke from high school—*lots of people have been turned to grape jelly there*. She continues along Alewife, passing Alewife Station on her right, and continues to Fresh Pond Mall, where she turns left. Threading her way through the shoppers, many there after work to knock off some Christmas shopping, Angie finds a place to park and goes into the McDonald's. *Familiar territory to review unfamiliar ground and write a story I don't know where it's going*, she thinks.

Keeping her eyes on the glossy picture-perfect menu above the uniformed and very bored-looking waitress, Angie orders a Quarter Pounder with cheese, large fries, a large Diet Coke, an apple pie, and then wends her way to a corner booth where she can spread out. She takes off her parka, sets her handbag on top of it on the seat next to her, sits with her back to the door, tucked in close to the wall. After unwrapping a burger and munching on an introductory fistful of fries, she takes her laptop out of her handbag with one hand and sets it on the table. Pressing its startup button and watching it flicker to life, she takes another handful of fries, bites off some more of her burger, washes it down with a long swallow of Diet Coke, and burps loudly before scrunching in her neck to make herself less exposed to anyone who might have heard her. Then she wipes her hands on her pants legs, realizing too late she is not in her accustomed jeans. She starts to write a story in Microsoft Word.

HOW I CAME TO WINK

By Angela Clarke
Special to the Advocate

This is not the story I was going to write. That story, about three murders and one very mysterious man presumed to be the murderer, never panned out. It might not be a news story either, because some of the things I am reporting here, while they happened, can't be fact-checked with multiple sourcing and documented chains of evidence. But what happened did happen and that's all there is to that. The most important thing, no matter who you are, or where you are, is what's going to happen next—awareness.

I met a number of young people who suffered from all sorts of diseases or disabilities while I was working on what I thought was going to be my prize-winning murder story. Brave children who lived—thrived, really—because of the love and support they received from adoring parents, siblings, and grandparents. The mothers, fathers, brothers, and sisters sometimes get forgotten in the course of treatments for the sick or disabled in their family. But they are disabled, too, in a way—disabled by proxy. They need love, acknowledgment, and care just as much as those who are sick or debilitated. These fellow sufferers need advocates, too. None of them—us—need sympathy, but some empathy? That would be nice.

There was one other person I never did meet, at least not in person, and this is his story, too. A man named Michael seemed to show up wherever I was looking, and I didn't know why. Michael spent time with the ill, the sickly, and the weak, and he gave them hope. He spent time with family members of those who were sick, and helped them help the children they loved. How he did it, whether he transferred energy from them to the sick kids they were helping, or whether that energy was there all along and he just facilitated it, I don't know. All I know is he did it and that I witnessed it.

The grandparents I had thought he was killing were all frail and dying as it turned out, and they all wanted so much to see their loved ones get well that they would have done anything to do so. And so, that's what they did. Michael helped them, and I don't have to know how. Faith, after all, believes without seeing. I saw the results in an old man's chair, a melting snowball on a cold winter's day, and that's enough for me.

Whatever your life experiences, they could all provide perspective. But at what point did my perspective go astray, not allowing me to notice the obvious? What factors caused me not to see, to not be able to look at things with fresh eyes each and every day? I'm not sure.

My perspective is forever changed now, and I hope everyone reading this will consider joining me in my soon-to- be-launched social awareness program I am calling "Wink." Why am I calling it that? It's mostly for personal reasons, but I don't mind explaining in broad brushstrokes why. As I traveled down this road on my way to a story that changed with every twist and turn in the path, I ran into a series of special people who were all seemingly trying to tell me something about whom I was supposed to become. In many cases, I heard them tell me things about letting go of preconceptions, about opening my heart and mind to the difficulties of others, and about the love and the energy contained in the interactions we all have with each other in the course of every day we spend on Earth. While I know I heard them all, I'm not so sure I was always really listening. And each one of my spirit guides on this journey seemed to realize this, and none of them judged me harshly for it. They just winked at me, usually as I was leaving their presence. You could call it a sign, or a salute, or a spiritual handshake—whatever you like. But whatever you want to call it, please remember what it means.

And what does "Wink" stand for? It stands for a belief system declaring that together, we as citizens of the world may effectuate change in how societies across the globe can support those children and their families who are stricken with life-threatening illnesses, or living with a disability of any type, by communicating the "Wink." Just tap your index finger to your thumb over your eye. Let it become the nonverbal, nonintrusive sign of support that will convey these basic premises:

- *we care*
- *they are not invisible*
- *their courageous example has touched our heart.*

I will be writing more about "Wink" in the near future, as I continue my exploration of the topic of people with disabilities and illnesses, and how best they and their families can be supported. Until next time.

Angie, having typed feverishly for over an hour, realizes where she is and how caught up she has become in her writing, and looks around her a little self-consciously. There are still people scattered at tables around her, but no one, including the waitstaff, looks to be the same people as when she first came in the restaurant. She looks to the side of her laptop, and sees the burger has seemingly grown tired of trying to look like its photograph in the glossy advertisement up on the wall. The fries, while also appearing tired and worn, do look slightly more edible, and she grabs three and maneuvers their twisted ends into her mouth. She looks back at the computer, saves her story, and makes a Wi-Fi connection to get into her gmail account. Upon opening it, she sees a message from jmi-nor@syr.edu—Jack. *I'm on a mission here, Jack, but you know I'm all ears where you're concerned*, she thinks. She opens it to read the five words that tell her everything she needs to know, the most she could wish to hear: "I miss you! Love, Jack." She feels warmth spread from her heart out to her fingers and toes, and she smiles. She pulls strands of hair from behind her left ear and dances the twisted wrap on the tip of her nose. Repressing an urge to reply too quickly, she waits for a full five seconds before replying, "Me, too, you!" and hitting the SEND button. *There*, she thinks. *That way, if he meant love like in just-a-friend love, I won't have exposed myself too much.*

Reenergized more by Jack's e-mail than by her din-ner—*now, this is a happy meal*, she thinks—Angie composes an e-mail to Bill Armstrong.

Hi Bill,

I am attaching a story based on my experience with the sledding deaths and where the story has taken off from there. It's probably more of a first-person op-ed piece than a news story, but I will leave that up to you. In the attached story, "How I Came to Wink," I sort of explain where I am with the story and where I'm going next, but I will be a little more specific with you.

My next stop is Give the Kids The World in Kissimmee, Florida, where I think I'll find this guy, Michael, who's been around the sledding deaths as well as around other people who have either had some sort of disability or illness. I don't think he's dangerous or a murderer or anything. As someone close to me said, I think he's a facilitator, some being who manages to transfer energy—dream energy—from someone with love in his or her heart, to another person less fortunate than they are from a physical standpoint. And this, in turn, allows the object of that love to feel and sense things they had previously not been able to sense or feel. I know that sounds vague and that's probably because I don't know, not yet, how it works. But I do know it's real because it's real; I've seen it in action. It's about love for those who are suffering, either in a physical sense or in the sense that they have to watch a loved one suffer.

Bill, you taught me a lot. The most important thing you taught me is to follow my instincts. That's what I'm doing. I'll write to you when I get to Florida, hopefully tomorrow.

Best,
Angie ("Lois Lane")

After hitting SEND and folding up her laptop, Angie decides she's had enough sitting and wants to get moving. It's been a long day and she just wants to check in with her parents and get some sleep. Then she can get up and book a flight for Florida. Getting all her stuff together, in a hurry now, Angie's up and out her booth as if practicing for a fire drill. Dumping what's left of her meal in the trash, she gets to the door and holds it for an older man struggling as he tries navigating his wheelchair through the breezeway. She offers him a smile, and he awards her one back, a moment of uncomplicated warmth and normalcy in a confusing and abnormal day.

She gets in her car, coaxes it to life. *Thank you, Bell. Hate to be stuck in a shopping mall, and what with my luck…*Then, careful to avoid the crush of people coming and going, she backs out and joins the ant army-like line of people converging on the mall's exit. She has to wait at the light for it to turn green, the consistently busy traffic flow made up of people leaving work late, going shopping, and those going out for the evening early. She takes a right, out onto Alewife Brook Parkway, ruminating about the name as she sees the sign. *I wonder if there's such a thing as an Alehusband for the Alewife? Maybe I should write a column about street names. That could be funny and satisfy the op-ed assignment for class. Good one, Ange.*

Angie feels content, fulfilled. She's worked her story hard, learned more than she thought possible, and made meaningful human connections. *If this is what growing up is like, at least some of the time, puberty and high school were worth it*, she thinks. Joining a snakelike string of red taillights winding its way up

Alewife, Angie is in no particular rush. Going with the flow, Angie is paying pretty close attention, knowing the rotary ahead will be a mess.

She doesn't make it through.

The 2009 Cadillac Esplanade that hits her comes careening out of Rindge Road, where it never even slowed at the stoplight. The SUV's driver, looking up from writing a text message to her husband on her Smartphone, turns her attention back to the road way too late to make a sweeping right turn onto Alewife. With its momentum barely diminished as it starts to slide, the SUV hits Angie's beloved Bell with a full broadside blow just behind the Accord's right front passenger door, caving it in on its way to causing what will lead to the real damage. Angie never sees what hits her; she just feels the impact too suddenly to be able to process what just happened.

Dr. Koogler, her Physics professor, would likely have been able to compute the force with which Bell and Angie, belted inside, were struck. A seventy-four-hundred-pound vehicle with cargo—two teenagers in the back and a mother preoccupied with texting on a cell phone in front—striking another vehicle weighing two thousand, seven hundred seventy-five pounds. With the estimated speed at which the SUV was traveling being forty-five miles per hour, according to the accident reconstruction report, the result of collision would be life changing – life ending. There would be several complicating factors at play in any Laws of Physics computation. For one thing, the Cadillac's center of gravity is higher than that of the Honda's center of gravity. This would keep the Honda from becoming airborne and this, in turn, would cause friction from the Honda's tires to resist the propelling violence of the Cadillac's impact, albeit minimally.

But given what happens next, Professor Koogler's initial equations attempting to apply the reality of physics to the force of the collision on Bell—and Angie—will be rendered moot. As the Cadillac forces the Honda into a fishtailing spin, its force continues to carry Bell, now held limp and helpless in the crushed grillwork of the much-larger Esplanade, into the oncoming lane of traffic that's heading south on Alewife. Having a green light, the Mello Fruit and Produce truck, a 1997 Isuzu N-Series, weighing fourteen thousand five hundred pounds and traveling forty miles per hour, slams into Bell's front, driver's side, now tilted at a forty-five-degree angle. The effect is like the violent clamping down of the hinged section of a steel trap suddenly sprung on an animal's leg.

The noises from the near-simultaneous crashes—the smash of the collision and the metal shrieking as it twisted; the screeching of the tires as their rubber is shorn off as it grinds against asphalt; the glass breaking, shattering, and then tinkling onto the roadway—Angie probably hears all of that. But she would be more disoriented by the loading up of g-forces as they knock her first one way, then unload in one nanosecond before another, opposing set of g-forces load up again on her body as she is struck the second time. Then all of those accumulated g-forces unload suddenly, violently.

Bell is now laid open like a gutted fish, split open at the passenger's side rear-door hinge by the compression of the westbound Esplanade, which functioned as anvil for the six-and-a-half-ton hammer that was the southbound Isuzu. When a hammer strikes an object being held at an angle—in this case, Bell is the object—against an anvil, the resultant energy has to be expended somewhere, which is why Bell split open in a place where it was not actually *struck* by anything. Cold air rushes into Bell's cavity, where it hisses as it runs over the superheated engine block that tore into the passenger compartment, which is where Angie's legs had just seconds before been resting comfortably as she worked the gas and brake pedals.

The pile of broken pieces, both vehicular and human, seems to sigh, as the whole mess settles and a weird hush falls on the accumulated shambles, like the silence before the claps of thunder when a severe storm blows through. In the lights, shards of glass from the windshields sparkle like rough-cut diamonds. Pieces of broken taillights glisten like spilled cherries.

Then the screams fill the silence. From the Esplanade, screams for help as its airbags settled. From the Isuzu, the driver, still shaken by the g-forces of the truck's sudden stop and the impact of its airbag, stumbles down from his cab. Shouts from other drivers as they get out of their cars to yell at each other to call 911. But from the Honda, nothing. Just Bell's radio still running the iPod accessory, playing Taylor Swift's "You Belong With Me." And Angie, covered with the now-deflated airbag and a large part of Bell's dashboard, one limp arm hanging out from underneath, over the center console. The engine block has burned through her pants to her skin, and the faint but pungent smell of burning meat rise upward toward her nostrils. Angie never smells a thing.

CHAPTER 16

The Call

Bill Armstrong's phone rings at home at 9:08. After nine o'clock he always picks up, as it's usually work-related, especially tonight. Reporters, daunted by the perceived importance of some item on the Tuesday evening Board of Selectmen meeting, and facing a deadline of noon the next day for their article submission, know it's better to ask questions early about how to proceed in coverage than to not ask at all. But the call isn't from a reporter with a question. It's from his paper's photographer, Pip Peters.

"Bill, it's Pip. I'm on an accident call I caught on the scanner. It's a three-vehicle, pretty bad, over by Alewife Station."

"Okay, Pip. Photoshop a few and put them on the server. I'll take a look in the morning. I don't have the whole front page laid out yet, so an accident will help. I'll get a reporter to pull the police report."

"Bill, it's not a regular accident. It's Angie." He's starting to sound shaken, trying to hold his voice from cracking.

"What?" Sharp, louder than intended. "What do mean, it's Angie?"

"I mean, it's Angie's car. It's beat up pretty bad."

"How is she? You talk to her?"

"No, Bill. She's gone."

"Gone? What does that mean, 'she's gone'?"

"They got her out with the Jaws and they took her in the ambulance."

"Where?"

"Mount Auburn Hospital."

"No coroner? There's still a chance."

"Bill, I don't think so." Pip knows Bill knows the drill—even when people are beyond repair, most ambulances will get the victims to the hospital so they can clear the paperwork and get back into service. Sending the coroner to the scene impedes this practical reality.

"All right. I'm on my way to the hospital."

"Bill?"

"Yeah?"

"I couldn't take any photographs. I froze. I know I should've, but I couldn't." He ends the sentence with the word "couldn't" sounding as if it's being squeezed by his voice box and compressed cheeks, as if he'd had a quick blast of helium. He starts to sob with the rhythm of a lawn mower coughing to a stop.

"It's all right, Pip. I would have had a hard time running them. A real hard time." Grief delivered suddenly with bluntness and tears are infectious. He has to hang up before he catches them.

The next few days are a blur for everyone. The paper gets out, although Bill leaves most of the layout and copyediting to his senior reporter. Funeral arrangements are made, friends of the family and of Angie flock to Arlington, and they try to console each other and make sense of such a needless death. The Clarkes begin their first quivering, confused, and tentative steps toward a life together with a giant hole in its center. The key for the filling in of the hole, and for the making sense of the senseless, turn up two days after the accident—the day of the funeral—in Bill Armstrong's e-mail. It has been there all along, left for Bill to find when he finally gets back to the routine of checking his inbox. He reads it and knows immediately what he must do.

But first, he indulges himself in his first real cry, a real cloud burster replete with peals of thunder and crackling electricity, in more than twenty years.

CHAPTER 17

Plane Water

The next morning, Bill's wife, Jean, drops him at the curb of Terminal E, where he's booked a flight to Orlando, Florida. Best known as the home of Disney, it is just as importantly the location of Give Kids the World. Bill gets out of the car, explains for the umpteenth time that this is a mission he needs to do solo, gives Jean a hug, bends down to unlock the telescopic arm of his luggage, and wheels it toward the Southwest entrance. A porter is methodically organizing another family's bags, loading the larger ones first, followed by the smaller ones. A middle-aged man, presumably the father, is feverishly writing out bag tags and ripping off previous ones from another airline carrier. The remaining members of the family—a mother, an older woman who is likely a grandmother, two boys, and a little girl—all exhibit various degrees of excitement, quite obviously about their pending excursion.

The little girl is about eleven years old, and she is spinning around in circles, half circles, and then back and forth in a kind of wheel-enabled dance routine. Her dance partner is a pink wheelchair, decorated with bright, shiny glitter and daisy stickers. Bill's eyes meet those of the little girl, who is having so much fun performing her intricate, practiced moves that it seems to be difficult for her to contain her enthusiasm. The older woman bends over and kisses the little girl on the right cheek, at which time she spins three hundred and sixty degrees counterclockwise to again lock eyes with Bill, who feels a little awkward but nonetheless smiles in her direction and offers a small nod. The little girl acknowledges the nod with one of her own, which she follows up with by raising her right hand toward her right eye, then tapping her right index finger and right thumb together twice, simultaneously winking. Bill turns around to see if the unusual gestures were for someone else, but he surmises instantly that he is the intended target. The little girl and her small entourage have moved inside the terminal and are now on their way, off to create new family memories.

"Can I help you, sir?" says a porter approaching from the service area.

"Oh, no, thanks, I'm fine. I'll check it inside."

Bill locates the nearest bank of flight departure-and-arrival screens and stands alongside other travelers, all of whom are arching their necks backward as if in the front seat of a movie theater. Bill reads the screens and sees his twelve o'clock flight to Orlando is on time, leaving out of gate 23A.

Soon his plane is next in line for takeoff, which is announced by the captain. The lift off is perfect, and as the plane slants to the south, Bill marvels at the beauty of the Boston skyline and the tiny tidiness of the city and its suburbs. *Seeing the world this way never gets old*, he thinks. *I wish it were Angie seeing this. Well, I'm just going to have to be the eyes to see her heart's vision through to completion. My eyes will have to see Michael for her. Am I up for asking him the right questions, though?*

Within two and a half hours, Bill finds himself on the ground, and, surprised at the fifty-degree difference in temperature, takes off his tie, loosens his collar, removes his sport coat, and drapes if over his arm as he wheels his luggage over to the taxi stand. "Give Kids the World, over in Kissimmee," he tells the cabbie as he enters the backseat of the cab.

Excited to be back in the field on a story, Bill feels the delicious mix of adrenaline, nervousness, and anticipation he used to feel as a reporter heading into unfamiliar territory.

The ride couldn't be quick enough. At times, he thinks he could probably run faster than the cab, which is actually traveling at the thirty-five-mile-per-hour speed limit. *Doesn't anybody speed anymore? Yeesh!* After a fitful, half-hour, stop-and-start journey past strip malls, condominium complexes, and service stations, Bill is ready to jump out of his skin.

As the cab approaches the entrance to the facility, Bill reminds himself of the sensitive nature of the story, noting he will have to practice some tact in his pursuit of fact, that Angie's analysis of this Michael character may or may not be accurate. *Trust your instincts, old-timer,* he tells himself, hoping those instincts haven't been dulled by years in the chair. The thought comes to him that he should remember the lessons and advice he had offered Angie. "Thanks for the reality check, Lois," he mutters under his breath with a half smile.

Emerging from the cab, he pays the driver and gives him a sizable tip. At the park entrance, the concierge, a medium-sized man in his twenties, tanned with brown, close-cropped hair, and sporting a white golf shirt with khaki shorts, is cheerfully greeting the new arrivals with a friendly smile. The organization's utility baseball player of sorts, he wears many hats and, with them, a variety of responsibilities. His two-way radio hangs handily on his belt, and like a gun-slinger in a dusty, cow-town street in a Western, he snatches it adeptly out of its holster, a tool for the practiced professional.

He blurts a few acronyms into the receiver, and then reverses his moves with the radio as he drops it back into its holster.

"Welcome!" he says, eyes sparkling as he reaches out to help Bill with his bags.

"Hi," Bill replies. "Um, I can handle the bags, thanks. I'm old but I'm not enfeebled."

"Sure, sir. Just stow them over in the shed over there on your way into the park. And welcome to Give Kids the World. How can I help you today?"

"I'm here to visit one of your staffers, a man named Michael." He removes the article featuring Michael and Give Kids the World from his briefcase.

The young man smiles and nods, a sense of pride clearly evident in his bearing.

"Wow! Wasn't that a great article? This is a great place. We're so proud of all our kids and Michael, too."

Bill acknowledges the greeter's excitement, but his reserve inhibits him from matching it, at least outwardly. "Do you know where I could find him? Michael, that is?"

"You know, you just missed him. He was here, not more than a few minutes ago. I think he was going to the pool area, but let me check where he might be. What is your name, please?"

Bill pauses, unaccustomed to being at a loss for words, and unsure of what introduction would be best. He knows the road to truth is best reached by practicing the truth and he decides to be forthright. "Bill Armstrong, from the *Arlington Advocate* in Arlington, Massachusetts. I'm here to do story on him, and on this place, as well," he says, spreading his free arm in an arc to indicate his intended objective.

The young man redraws his radio, clicks the receiver, and speaks into it.

"Jessie, hi, it's Gus. You know where Michael is? I have a gentleman here that wants to chat with him, from the *Arlington Advocate* newspaper." He waits, listening to a response. "Wasn't he poolside not too long ago?"

Bill, never really patient despite his outward demeanor, is having trouble containing himself, shifting from one foot to the other. He idly considers the wisdom of skipping the formalities and rushing past this well-intentioned bundle of enthusiasm, straight into the facility to take over the search on his own. The young enthusiasm bundle waits again for the response. "Got it. Yeah. OK. Thanks."

The greeter seems relieved with the answer from other party on the two-way, reholsters his radio, and looks back at Bill with a friendly smile. "You're all set, Mr. Armstrong. He's just over there," he says, pointing over his right shoulder with his thumb. "At the aquatic center, working with a couple of kids. You see this King Triton's trident right here?" he asks, looking down at a painted image of a half-human, half-fish bearded man holding a three-pronged spear on the pathway. "You just follow that, and you'll be all set. Okay?"

Bill nods, wheels his luggage over to the nearby storage shed, and sets off on his given—or acquired—mission. The trident path twists and turns, and as he walks deeper into this special place, he begins to hear the laughter of children and music. The pungent smell of chlorine hits his nose, so he knows the pool must be near. Through the gaps of a tall hedge, he sees someone who looks as if he could be Michael. He stops and peers toward the figure by the edge of the pool. As he watches, the man turns and Bill is sure. Almost at the same instant as Bill makes the recognition, the man, Michael, notices him as well and their eyes lock.

The corners of Michael's mouth rise, shooting a friendly, slightly ironic smile in Bill's direction. It's a smile that says, "I know why you're here" but is also a smile with a hint of sorrow at its corners, as if also saying, "I'm sorry it has to be you here instead of…"

Angie. Bill thinks of her immediately, and so energized, he moves down the hedge line slowly at first, then more quickly, moving from a relatively unobstructed vantage spot on his side of the hedge to another, more hidden one about twenty yards farther down the path. He pulls back the branches like a child tentatively pulling back the curtain at a grade school play to say hi to his parents. He continues this small act, feeling a little silly but unable to contain himself as he moves along the path. Michael remains still as he tracks Bill's progress, watching his movements intently with a bemused smile, as if silently cheering him on.

Finally Bill can't restrain himself any longer and rushes to end of the hedge with a series of long strides performed at the pace of a quick walk, expecting to see Michael standing there in the open, awaiting a confrontation. But he's gone. Bill sees the back half of Michael's right leg as he disappears, turning the corner around a poolside cabana. The speed at which the leg disappears indicates to Bill he is likely moving at a full run. He rushes after him, leaving adult inhibitions behind, fueled by adrenaline. Hampered by his loosely fastened sandals, his first few steps are clumsy. But summoning track out of his distant past, he breaks into a full sprint, knees rising and falling like pistons, chest and head upright as he cuts corners around poolside chairs, tables, and bathers. As he rounds the cabana, the path splits and it's decision time—*left or right?* Bill stops and turns his head both ways, listening like an assassin for any hint of which way Michael may have gone. From the path to the right, he hears the rumble of what sounds like a motorcycle, a loud rumbling Harley Davidson. He takes a few steps in that direction, just in time to see the retreating yellow of Michael's T-shirt through the bushes alongside an adjacent street to the park. *Damn!* In anger, he kicks a clump of roses by the path, causing some of its petals to explode.

Bill rests his hands on his knees, bent over and still gasping. He lets his rapid panting slow to a normal breathing rate and stands up straight, still tasting the coppery taste of blood-engorged lungs. In the direction of the path to the left, over a shallow row of rosebushes, he can see off in the distance a little girl sitting in a wheelchair, slightly in the shade of an overhanging dogwood tree. Something draws Bill in the direction of the little girl, whom he had seen earlier. The landscape along the path is adorned with prickly rosebushes and small ornamental trees, occasionally interrupting his view. There are some slight inclines in and around the garden area. At one point, Bill loses sight of her, as there are some vibrant flowering lantanas obstructing his view. As Bill makes what he thinks is the final turn, he expects to see the little girl but she is not there. Just her wheelchair remains.

Where did she…? How did she…? I just saw her.

Bill stops, looks around, and even retraces a couple steps. Curious, he jogs back to the vantage point from which he saw her last, but only the wheelchair remains. Bill treads back down the path and comes next to the wheelchair. There's a fresh-looking puddle by its base. He dips a finger in the puddle and brings it to his nose and sniffs it for a scent, of which there is none.

Water? Plain water?

Then Bill spies its trail. His eyes follow a thin line of water up a rise, around a bend, to a low wall where the girl is sitting. She is a beautiful girl, with shiny brown hair, who looks to be about nine years old. She is wearing a floral summer dress with a matching beret. Her eyes are closed, and there is a wide, bright smile on her face. She appears to be visualizing something, as her head moves from side to side in a figure eight and her eyes seem to be dancing under her eyelids. Then the little girl's eyes slowly open, as if from a dreamy state, to meet Bill's. He averts his gaze from the girl's stare, and is embarrassed he might have interrupted a private moment. Then he slowly returns his eyes to meet the girl's once again. The little girl *winks* at Bill, as she displays the American Sign Language sign for wink with her two tiny fingers. Bill, summoning Angie in his mind's eye again, politely smiles and returns the wink signal with his right hand.

He bends to be at eye level with the little girl. "You're imagining something fun, huh?" he asks in a whisper.

The little girl nods. She's still smiling and lowers her eyes to Bill's left foot, which obstructs the stream, the water tickling around the front outline of his shoes, dribbling to the back of his heel. He lifts and flexes his shoe, making micro splashes. Sharing a light moment, they both laugh. The little girl's giggling stops, followed by a curious and knowing smile. Together, Bill's and the little girl's gaze slowly follows the course the water has traveled, until their eyes settle on its source, lying between the little girl's feet—a pure white melting snowball. A gift.

"Oh, Angie," Bill says softly to himself. "You knew so much more than you knew you knew." He knows he has enough pent-up emotion to wash away the puddle of snow that melted this little girl's heart by rounding out a dream, but he holds it in. He needs to channel them, put them to good use.

CHAPTER 18

Doorway to Awareness

Back in Arlington two days later, and facing down the end of another weekly news cycle, Bill flips on his office computer, waits for it to wake, and opens a Word document as blank and empty as a winter whiteout. The curser appears and disappears, a vertical line daring him to start and make thoughts stick to the screen. He takes up the challenge:

> *Edit/12/24/2011*
>> *Header: Passing along a Wink and a Prayer*

For years too many to mention, I've written editorials on this page that have tended to focus on several overall themes. Many have centered on power and its myriad number of applications, as it is wielded for either light or dark purposes, and how those applications affect us as citizens. Many have congratulated or castigated people in those seats of power and influence. To some degree or other, virtually all editorials have centered on recent achievements or failures—or potential failures—of the people who are in the public eye.

This one won't be like those. Readers know about the recent and needless death of one of our town's bright lights, Angela "Angie" Clarke. The fact she was an intern here, while important to note, is only part of Angie's importance to me, to us, and, without exaggeration, to the world at large. Weighty words, those. It's been left to me to explain, and I will, to the best of my ability, why that is the case. Those of you who are familiar with my work might be surprised to know this, but I have feelings. I don't mind saying that tears have calloused the paths on my cheeks these last few days, finding my way back to reality. I have a spiritual side, one allowing me to tap into a power greater than myself, although I shrink from any ostentatious, showy displays of faith. My belief is just that—my belief. And this is what I believe.

I believe Angie Clarke was given a mission. While she may not have seen the end of that mission, she was beginning to plot its destination. Ms. Clarke had uncovered a road map to a better place for a group of unrecognized people, perhaps the last tribe of underrepresented groups on this planet: the disabled and their caregivers, families, and loved ones. Last week's issue of the Arlington Advocate contained Ms. Clarke's last article, in which she wrote impassionedly about the struggles, trials, and tribulations of children who suffer from some sort of disability, which was a timely, necessary, and important message to impart. But Ms. Clark did not stop there. She went farther with her eloquent empathy, farther than most adults are capable, and that is what was truly amazing about this young journalist. She wrote about how the families—the brothers, sisters, parents, and grandparents—struggle along with the one with the illness, disease, or affliction. It was a remarkable revelation for anyone to have, much less a young person on the cusp of adulthood.

Some people would say that God's will is an easy enough thing to say when it's not them who is disabled or afflicted. Maybe that's true, maybe it isn't. For me, someone who was devastated by the loss of this young lady, I know it is true. I believe God's grace put me here to tell Ms. Clarke's— okay, Angie's—story. Angie's vision was one that most likely would have taken her outside of the journalism pro-fession. That would have been a great loss for the profession, but she had a vision for an overall idea, a concept that would have charted a new sort of philanthropy for the disabled, one that would have been a more inclusive and humanistic methodology for treating, interacting with, and tending to the disabled and their families. Her vision was to establish a two-way communication, the sign of a wink, a conduit between their world and our world, the world of the healthy, or, as we selfishly perceive it, the world of the normal.

There is an Old English proverb, "The eyes are the windows to the soul," so perhaps a wink will become the doorway to greater awareness. So fresh and clean, her core message of awareness will bring these two worlds together. I know it. Anything is possible, even a melting snowball in the Florida sun.

CHAPTER 19

Signs

Four years later
    The Clarkes' Volvo exits their street, leaving Spy
Pond in their rearview mirror. Cliff's deep breaths, the rise
and fall of his chest, are accentuated by his freshly pressed
orange shirt. Sue's left hand reaches down and rests on his
right knee for a second, and she gives it a tender squeeze.
They look at each other and smile. Sue pulls down the passenger side mirror from the visor and adjusts an orange pin
on her jacket. From the backseat, Marcie's mother places her

hand on Sue's shoulder, offering support. Marcie's parents share a private look across the backseat.

At the light, Cliff turns right onto Massachusetts Avenue and proceeds through Arlington Center. It's dusk and there is moderately heavy traffic, due to the usual Saturday church service traffic leaving St. Agnes, as well as the dinner-hour traffic going to, and departing from, the local restaurants. About a mile out of Arlington Center, Cliff begins to slow down and pulls to the curb, as the red brake lights of traffic ahead reflect off the front hood into the windshield. The foursome exits the car, with Cliff waiting for Sue to join him on the curb. He takes her hand and walks along the sidewalk in the direction of Arlington's historic Capitol Theatre. They are returning to a place frequented by their dear Angie in her youth, when Cliff or Sue typically waited in the car for drop-offs and pickups of Angie and her friends.

Tonight is different, but a sense of familiarity jogs their memories and subsequently unlocks their subconscious emotions. In a signal of comfort, Cliff squeezes Sue's hand with a single pump, and Sue responds with two pumps of her own. They repeat the pattern, keeping in pace with each other's footsteps along the aged brick sidewalk.

For a city block, the environment around the Capitol Theatre is transformed on this single evening into the setting of a Hollywood movie premiere. The bright beams of searchlights strobe across the sky, and the outbursts of dueling police whistles seem to mimic the white-gloved hand flashes of the officers directing traffic and signaling for pedestrians to cross. Sue's pace quickens, and she pulls Cliff's arm abruptly at the sight of a tall young man looking as if he has lost someone among the crowd. "Jack, honey, over here," calls Sue. Jack Minor, looking dapper as ever, sporting the same shirt as Cliff, moves through the crowd and hugs both Cliff and Sue. He pulls back to see their beaming faces. "This is amazing, isn't it?" says Jack. Sue and Cliff's faces mirror Jack's excitement, relying on the emotions of the moment to carry them along. "She did all this!" says Jack. "She did it!"

"Hey, orange looks good on you, pal," says Cliff.

"Aren't these great? Sue, you did an awesome job on the 'Wink' design," replies Jack. Sue smiles and hugs him again.

Like many who loved her, they bear heavy hearts, but are thankful for the time they shared with their loving Angie, who is being posthumously honored with the debut of *Wink*, the motion picture. They file among a capacity crowd and sit in the rear left side of the theater. Sue is looking at the cascading rows of packed seats and envisioning that if her daughter were there, she would be right in the mix of it, picking her way around the wheelchairs, handing out boxes of popcorn, sharing and celebrating with the children she served to protect and honor. "She would have loved this, Cliff," says Sue, trying to hold back tears. Cliff pats Sue's hand and kisses her cheek, buying time to give a controlled response. "She's with us, Mommy. She's with us." His voice cracks as he chokes out the words.

They long for the film to go on, hoping for it to never end as they feel her connection, her spirit—something they have missed and longed for in the stark reality of life.

The reflection of the closing scene washes over the faces in the audience, and the inspirational soundtrack pumps from the cinema speakers. Pictures flash up on screen of the real-life Wink charitable efforts promoting awareness that have taken place across the world, pictures of Angie from a few years ago are among them. A "Wink" music video starts to play, showing real-life images of the incredible kids and their families. It displays them during holidays and while conquering obstacles such as skiing, sledding, horseback riding, and just having fun with friends. Famous musicians, bands, athletes, and actors are shown rocking out to the "Wink" video. Celebrities are shown making eye contact with the children and their families, doing the Wink. The atmosphere is fun and light and moviegoers practice doing the Wink as they leave their seats and file out of the theater into the lobby.

As several teenagers exit into the stillness of the hallway, they see a boy about their age, walking alone with a walker, who is coming from the other exit. They look at each and change their direction so they are in line with his.

"Let's go," says one of the kids. As they approach the boy with the walker, they make eye contact and flash the Wink, which he returns with a smile.

"Hey, what's your name?" asks one of the kids in the group.

"Sam," he replies.

"Well, it's good to meet you, man," another kid says.

"Hey, we're gonna grab a soda and play some video at the arcade in the lobby. Why don't you hang with us?" says another.

Sam smiles, looks back at his mother, who is making her way over from the exit of the theater. She nods, as if to say, "Go ahead." Sam's brightened face quickly returns to the kids.

"Yeah, sure. Cool," he says.

"Awesome," the kids reply.

EPILOGUE

*M*om, Dad, Jack, and all my Wink supporters—I hope you realize this message in your dreams. I love you all very much, but don't worry about me. I'm perfectly fine, just miss you and I know you me. You know time moves in funny ways, ways I was not aware of. And now I've let go of the reins to you, the adopters of my awareness message, Wink. It is incredible to think that Wink is not only a book, but—dare I say it?—a movement, and now this movie. Way to go, gang, and I love the website, wink2support.com! I encourage everyone to please check it out, and help promote its awareness message.

It's the movement that makes me the proudest. Seeing you guys sign the Wink as symbols of "I get you," support, and caring makes me feel fulfilled. By embracing the story of the Wink, you have

embraced a movement that allows for everyone—not just the beautiful, the whole, and the perfectly healthy—to take a seat at the table
and be relevant.

It has made the world a nicer, kinder, and richer place to look
upon, I can tell you that.

Peace,
Angela (Angie) Clarke

THE END

Proof

Made in the USA
Charleston, SC
15 March 2013